13

Also edited by James Howe

The Color of Absence: 12 Stories About Loss and Hope

13

Thirteen
stories that
capture the
agony and
ecstasy
of being
thirteen

edited by JAMES HOWE

ATHENEUM BOOKS FOR YOUNG READERS
NEW YORK LONDON TORONTO SYDNEY SINGAPORE

For Amy Berkower

TABLE OF CONTENTS

Introduction 1
James Howe

What's the Worst That Could Happen? 7
Bruce Coville

Kate the Great 29
Meg Cabot

If You Kiss a Boy 49
Alex Sanchez

Thirteen and a Half 75
Rachel Vail

Jeremy Goldblatt Is *So* Not Moses 89
James Howe

Black Holes and Basketball Sneakers 115
Lori Aurelia Williams

Picky Eater 161
Stephen Roos

Such Foolishness 181
Maureen Ryan Griffin

Noodle Soup for Nincompoops 187
Ellen Wittlinger

Squid Girl 213
Todd Strasser

Angel & Aly 229
Ron Koertge

Nobody Stole Jason Grayson 251
Carolyn Mackler

Tina the Teen Fairy 267
Ann M. Martin and Laura Godwin

INTRODUCTION

James Howe

I was in the eighth grade when I was thirteen. I had moved the year before from a small town where, despite my complete lack of athletic ability, I was popular enough to be voted "Most Likely to Grow Up to Become President of the United States." Now I lived in a country-club suburb where it was made clear my first day of school that I didn't have what it took to be "in." I spent a lot of time asking questions: What's wrong with me? Why am I different? What does it take to be popular? What are the rules? Who decides them?

Not surprisingly, many of the stories in this collection ask these very same questions, and almost every one of them uses school either as its setting or as an important reference point in the main character's life.

While school may be the main stage on which being thirteen is played out, it is only the backdrop to the drama itself. If you are thirteen, almost thirteen, or have ever been thirteen, you know the drama I'm talking about. Suddenly, your body is going through weird and surprising changes. The face staring back at you from the mirror looks different (usually worse) from one day to the next. You find yourself paying attention to the opposite—or same—sex with a new and often confusing intensity. Your moods swing. Your friendships are put through tests and sometimes barely survive (and sometimes don't survive at all). Your parents embarrass you simply by breathing. (Do they have to be so *obvious* about it? And why do they insist on *humming* in public?) You need privacy, a simple fact that certain people just don't seem to get. You think about things in ways you never have before—*big* things, like life and death, religion, God, love, racism, sexism, politics, the environment, what it means to be rich or poor, what it means to be a friend, what it means to be an adult, what it means to be leaving your childhood behind.

"I felt like I was on a boat: off balance and kind of lurchy/nauseated, though excited," Rachel Vail writes about her experience of being thirteen. "And although I was eager to get where I was going . . . it was also difficult to watch my familiar childhood world grow more distant and less my own as I pulled away from its safe shore."

In the stories you are about to read, the main characters are all pulling away from that safe shore, going through the changes and asking the questions that make thirteen the unique time in life that it is. Of course, twelve stories and one poem can cover only a limited range of experiences. None may reflect your life in its particulars, but there's a good chance that all of them will in one way or another reflect your feelings—the experiences of your heart, mind, and soul.

I hope your pleasure in reading this book will come close to the pleasure I had in working with these outstanding writers. What incredible luck that twelve of my favorite young-adult authors and one of my favorite poets all said yes to contributing an original piece of writing to this collection. And what questions they ask:

> "If thirteen is supposed to be an unlucky number, what does it mean that we are forced to go through an entire year with that as our age?"
>
> "Why is it so hard to accept someone who is so different?"
>
> "Was he wrong to want the sneakers that all the other kids had?"
>
> "Why is it so pervie to kiss another guy?"
>
> "I think you can tell a lot about a person by the way she eats Mallomars, don't you?"
>
> "Haven't you learned *anything* about boys?"
>
> "What the heck is going on here?"

That last question (from Bruce Coville's "What's the Worst That Could Happen?") just about sums it all up, doesn't it? As Maia Grant discovers in "Tina the Teen Fairy," by Ann M. Martin and Laura Godwin, being thirteen is just the beginning of a time of questioning, confusion, and discovery. But it is also a time that provides an opportunity to try on identities, to find oneself, and to explore the biggest question of all: Who am I?

In the end, this book may offer more questions than answers. But then, so does life. Using Rachel Vail's boat metaphor, if answers are the destination (and destinations are always changing), questions are the oars.

Read.

Grab an oar or two.

And set sail.

What's the Worst That Could Happen?

Bruce Coville

If thirteen is supposed to be an unlucky number, what does it mean that we are forced to go through an entire year with that as our age? I mean, you would think a civilized society could just come up with a way for us to skip it.

Of course, good luck and I have rarely shared the same park bench. Sometimes I think Murphy's Law—you know, "If something can go wrong, it will"—was invented just for me. I suppose the fact that my name is Murphy Murphy might have something to do with that feeling.

Yeah, you read it right: Murphy Murphy. It's like a family curse. The last name I got from my father, of course. The first name came down from my mother's side, where it is a tradition for the firstborn son. You would think my mother might have considered that before she married Dad, but love makes fools of us all, I guess. Anyway, the fact that I got stuck with the same name coming and going, so to speak, shows that my parents are either spineless (my theory) or have no common sense (my sister's theory).

I would like to note that no one has ever apologized to me for this name. "I think it's lovely," says my mother—which, when you consider it, would seem to support my sister's theory. Anyway, you can see that right from the beginning of my life, if something could go wrong, it did.

Okay, I suppose it could have been worse. I could have been born dead or with two heads or something. On the other hand, as I lie here in my hospital bed trying to work out exactly how I got here, there are times when I wonder if being born dead might not have been the best thing.

To begin with, I want to say here and now that Mikey Farnsworth should take at least part of the blame for this situation. This, by the way, is true for many of the bad things that have happened in my life, from the paste-eating incident in first grade through the bogus fire-drill situation last year, right up to yesterday afternoon, which was sort of the Olympics of Bad Luck as far as I'm concerned. What's amazing is that somehow Mikey ends up coming out of these things looking perfectly fine. He is, as my grandfather likes to say, the kind of guy who can fall in a manure pile and come out smelling like a rose.

The one I am not going to blame is Tiffany Grimsley, though if I hadn't had this stupid crush on her, it never would have happened.

Okay, I want to stop and talk about this whole thing of having a crush. Let me say right up front that it is very confusing and not something I am used to. When it started, I was totally baffled. I mean, I don't even like girls, and all of a sudden I keep thinking about one of them? Give me a break!

In case it hasn't happened to you yet, let me warn you. Based on personal experience, I can say that while there are many bad things about having a crush, just about the worst of them is the stupid things you will do because of it.

Okay, let's back up here.

I probably wouldn't even have known I had a crush to begin with if Mikey hadn't informed me of this fact. "Man, you've got it bad for Tiffany," he says one day when we are poking around in the swamp behind his house.

"What are you talking about?" I ask. At the same time, my cheeks begin to burn as if they are on fire. Startled, I lift my foot to tie my shoe, which is a trick I learned in an exercise magazine and that has become sort of a habit. At the moment, it is mostly an excuse to look down.

What the heck is going on here? I think.

Mikey laughs. "Look at you blush, Murphy! There's no point in trying to hide it. I watched you drooling over her in social studies class today. And you've only mentioned her, like, sixteen times since we got home this afternoon."

"Well, sure, but that's because she's a friend," I say,

desperately trying to avoid the horrible truth. "We've known each other since kindergarten, for Pete's sake."

Mikey laughs again, and I can tell I'm not fooling him. "What am I going to do?" I groan.

He shrugs. "Either you suffer in silence, or you tell her you like her."

Is he nuts? If you tell a girl you like her, it puts you totally out in the open. I mean, you've got no place to hide. And there are really only two possible responses you're going to get from her: (a) She likes you, too, which the more you think about it, the more unlikely it seems; or (b) anything else, which is, like, totally, utterly humiliating. I'm sure girls have problems of their own. But I don't think they have any idea of the sheer terror a guy has to go through before any boy-girl stuff can get started.

I sure hope this gets easier with time, because I personally really don't understand how the human race has managed to survive this long, given how horrifying it is to think about telling a girl you like her.

Despite Mikey's accusation, I do not think I have actually drooled over Tiffany during social studies class. But it is hard not to think about her then, because she sits right in front of me. It's the last class of the day, and the October sunlight comes in slantwise and catches in her golden hair in a way that makes it hard to breathe.

It does not help that eighth-grade social studies is taught by Herman Fessenden, who you will probably see on the front of the *National Enquirer* someday as a mass murderer for boring twenty-six kids to death in a single afternoon. It hasn't happened yet, but I'm sure it's just a matter of time.

I spend the entire weekend thinking about what Mikey has said, and I come up with a bold plan, which is to pass Tiffany a note asking if she wants to grab a slice of pizza at Angelo's after school. I am just getting up my nerve to do it—there are only five minutes of class left—when Mr. F. says, "So, what do you think the queen should have done then, Murphy?"

How am I supposed to know? But I blush and don't hand the note to Tiffany after all, which wouldn't have been so bad, except that Butch Coulter saw I had it and grabs it on the way out of class, and I have to give him the rest of my week's lunch money to get it back.

Tuesday I try a new tactic. There's a little store on the way to school where you can pick up candy and gum and stuff, and I get some on the way to school and then kind of poke Tiff in the back during social studies class, which is about the only time I see her, to ask if she wants a piece of gum. Only before she can answer, Mr. Fessenden comes up from behind and snatches the whole pack out of my hand. So that was that.

Then, on Wednesday, it's as if the gods are smiling on me, which is not something I am used to. Tiffany grabs my arm on the way out of social studies and says, "Can I talk to you for a second, Murphy?"

"Sure," I say. This is not very eloquent, but it is better than the first thought that crosses my mind, which is, "Anytime, anywhere, any moment of the day." It is also better than, "Your words would be like nectar flowing into the hungry mouths of my ears," which was a line I had come up with for a poem I was writing about her.

She actually looks a little shy, though what this goddess-on-Earth has to be shy about is more than I can imagine.

She hands me a folded-over set of papers, and my heart skips a beat. Can this be a love letter? If so, it's a really long one.

"I wrote this skit for drama club, and I thought maybe you would do it with me next Friday. I think you'd be just right for the part."

My heart starts pounding. While it seems unlikely that the part is that of a barbarian warrior prince, just doing it means I will have an excuse to spend time with Tiffany. I mean, we'll have to rehearse and . . . well, the imagination staggers.

"Yes!" I say, ignoring the facts that (a) I have not yet read the script and (b) I have paralyzing stage fright.

She gives me one of those sunrise smiles of hers, grabs my arm and gives it a squeeze, and says, "Thanks. This is going to be fun." Then she's gone, leaving me with a memory of her fingers on my arm and a wish that I had started pumping iron when I was in first grade, so my biceps would have been ready for this moment.

Mikey moves in a second later. "Whoa," he says, nudging me with his elbow. "Progress! What did she say?"

"She wants me to do a skit with her."

He shakes his head. "Too bad. I thought maybe

you had a chance. How'd she take it when you told her no?"

I look at him in surprise. "I didn't. I said I would do it."

Mikey looks even more surprised. "Murphy, you can't go onstage with her. You can't even move when you get onstage. Don't you remember what happened in fifth grade?"

As if I could forget. Not only was it one of the three most humiliating moments of my life, but according to my little brother, it has become legendary at Westcott Elementary. Here's the short version: Mrs. Carmichael had cast me as George Washington in our class play, and I was, I want to tell you, pretty good during rehearsals. But when they opened the curtain and I saw the audience . . . well, let's just say that when my mother saw the look on my face, she actually let out a scream. She told me later she thought I was having a heart attack. As for me, my mouth went drier than day-old toast, some mysterious object wedged itself in my throat, and the only reason I didn't bolt from the stage was that I couldn't move my arms or legs. Heck, I couldn't even move my fingers.

I couldn't even squeak!

Finally, they had to cancel the performance. Even after the curtains were closed, it took two teachers and a janitor to carry me back to the classroom.

"This time will be different," I say.

Mikey snorts.

I know he is right. "Oh, man, what am I gonna do?" I wail.

"Come on, let's look at the script. Maybe all you have to do is sit there and she'll do all the acting."

No such luck. The script, which is called "Debbie and the Doofus," is very funny.

It also calls for me to say a lot of lines.

It also calls for me to act like a complete dork.

Immediately, I begin to wonder why Tiffany thinks I would be just right for this role.

"Maybe she imagines you're a brilliant actor," says Mikey.

He is trying to be helpful, but to tell the truth, I am not sure which idea is worse: that Tiffany thinks I am a dork or that she thinks I am a brilliant actor.

"What am I gonna do?" I wail again.

"Maybe your parents will move before next week," says Mikey, shaking his head. "Otherwise, you're a dead man walking."

I ask, but my parents are not planning on moving.

I study the script as if it is the final exam for life, which as far as I am concerned, it is. After two days I know not only my lines, but all of Tiffany's lines, too, as well as the lines for Laurel Gibbon, who is going to be playing the waitress at the little restaurant where we go for our bad date.

My new theory is that I will enjoy rehearsals and the excuse they give me to be with Tiffany, and then pray for a meteor to strike me before the day of the performance.

The first half of the theory actually seems to work. We

have two rehearsals—one at school and one in Tiffany's rec room. At the first one she is very impressed by the fact that I know my lines already. "This is great, Murphy!" she says, which makes me feel as if I have won the lottery.

At the second rehearsal I actually make Laurel, who is perhaps the most solemn girl in the school, laugh. This is an amazing sound to me, and I find that I really enjoy it. Like Tiffany, Laurel has been in our class since kindergarten. Only I never noticed her much because, well, no one ever notices Laurel much, on account of she basically doesn't talk. I wondered at first why Tiffany had cast her, but it turns out they are in the same church group and have been good friends for a long time.

Sometimes I think the girls in our class have a whole secret life that I don't know about.

Time becomes very weird. Sometimes it seems as if the hours are rushing by in a blur, the moment of performance hurtling toward me. Other times the clock seems to poke along like a sloth with chronic fatigue syndrome. Social studies class consists of almost nothing but staring at the sunshine in Tiffany's hair and flubbing the occasional question that Mr. Fessenden lobs at me. Some days I think he asks me questions out of pure meanness. Other days he leaves me alone, and I almost get the impression he feels sorry for me.

Mikey and I talk about the situation every night. "No meteor yet," he'll say, shaking his head.

"What am I gonna do?" I reply, repeating the question

that haunts my days. I can't possibly tell Tiffany I can't do this.

"Maybe you could be sick that day?" says Mikey.

I shake my head. "If I let her down, I will hate myself forever."

Mikey rolls his eyes. "Maybe you should run away from home," he suggests, not very helpfully.

Finally, we do come up with a plan, which is that Mikey will stay in the wings to prompt me in case the entire script falls out of my head. I don't know if this will really do much good, since if I freeze with terror, mere prompting will not be of any use. On the other hand, knowing Mikey will be there calms me down a little. It's like having a life jacket.

Ha! Little do I know what kind of life jacket he will turn out to be.

To my dismay, I have not been able to parlay my time working on the skit with Tiffany into anything bigger. This is partly because she is the busiest person in the eighth grade, with more clubs and committees and activities than any normal person could ever be involved with. It is also because I am stupid about this kind of thing and don't have the slightest clue how to do it. So I treasure my memory of the two rehearsals and, more than anything else, the sound of her laughing at some of what I have done.

Despite my prayers, Friday arrives. I don't suppose I really expected God to cancel it, though I would have been deeply appreciative if he had. I go through the day in a state of cold terror. The drama club meeting is after school. Members of the club have invited their friends, their families, and some teachers to come see the skits. There are going to be four skits in all. Tiffany, Laurel, and I are scheduled to go last, which gives me more time to sweat and worry.

Mikey is backstage with us, but Tiffany does not know why. I tell her he came because he is my pal. Getting him aside, I check to make sure he has the script.

At 2:45 Mrs. Whitcomb, the drama club coach, comes back to wish us luck. She makes a little speech, which she ends with, "Okay, kids—break a leg!"

This, of course, is how people wish each other luck in the theater. According to my mother, the idea is that you're not going to get your wish anyway, so you wish for the thing you don't want and you may get the thing you do want instead.

I suddenly wonder if this is what I have been doing wrong all my life.

On the other hand, Tiffany is standing next to me, so that is one wish that is continuing to come true.

"Are you excited?" she asks.

"You have no idea," I answer, with complete honesty.

Laurel, who is standing on the other side of me, whispers, "I'm scared."

"Don't worry, you'll be fine," I reply.

I am fairly confident this is true, since I expect to make such an ass of myself that no one will notice anything else anyway. Inside me, a small voice is screaming, "What were you thinking of, you moron? You are going to humiliate yourself in front of all these people, including the girl you would cut out your heart for, who will be even more humiliated than you are because it's her skit that you are messing up! Run away! Run away!"

If I could get my hands on this small voice, I would gladly beat it to a bloody pulp. Instead, I keep taking deep breaths and reminding myself of how funny I was during the rehearsals.

The first skit goes up. I think it's funny, but at first no one laughs. This terrifies me all over again. Then someone snickers. A moment later someone else lets out a snort. Pretty soon everyone is laughing. Clearly, it takes people a while to get warmed up when they are trying to have fun.

At first the sound of that laughter is soothing. But it takes only a few minutes for me to get terrified by it. What if they don't laugh at *our* skit? Even worse, what if they laugh for the wrong reasons? What if Tiffany is totally humiliated, and it's all my fault?

I go back to wanting to die.

The second skit goes up and dies in my place. It just lies onstage, stinking the place up like a week-old fish. It's as boring as last month's newspaper. In fact, it's almost as boring as Mr. Fessenden, which I would not have thought possible. I feel a surge of hope. We can't look worse than this. In fact, next to it we'll seem like geniuses. Too bad we can't go on right away!

Unfortunately, we have to wait for the third skit, which turns out to be brilliant, which makes me want to kill the people who are in it. Now we'll be compared to them instead of the dead fish of that second skit.

The curtain closes.

"Our turn," whispers Tiffany. "Break a leg, Murphy."

"Break a leg," I murmur back. Then, so Laurel won't feel left out, I say the same thing to her as we pick up the table that is our main prop and move it onto the stage. Tiffany is right behind us with a pair of chairs. Once they're in place, we scurry to our positions, Tiffany and me stage right, Laurel stage left.

My stomach clenches. Cold sweat starts out on my brow.

"Murphy!" hisses Tiffany. "Your shoelace!"

I glance down. I have forgotten to untie it, which is the key to one of my first funny bits. Out of habit, I lift my foot to take care of the lace. At that instant the curtain opens, which startles me so much that I lose my balance and fall over, landing onstage in full view of the audience.

There they are. The enemy. The people who are going to stare at me, judge me, whisper about me tomorrow. I am so frozen with terror I cannot move. I just lie there looking at them.

And then the laugh begins. My temperature goes in two directions, my blood turning to ice at the same time that the heat rises in my face. I have a long moment of terror—well, it feels like a long moment; according to

Mikey, it was less than two seconds—while I think that this is it, I will never stand up again, never come to school again, never leave my house again. I will ask whoever finally picks me up to carry me home and put me in the attic. My parents will have to shove my meals through a slot in the door because I will never be able to face another living human being.

Love saves the day. "Murphy, are you all right?" hisses Tiffany.

For the sound of that voice, I would do anything—even get back on my feet.

And then, the second miracle. Some brilliant portion of my brain realizes that this is a comedy and I have just started us off with a big laugh. I stand at the edge of the stage to do a fake knock. In rehearsal, I only mimed it. Now, for some reason, I say loudly, "Knock-knock. Knockity-knock-knock."

To my surprise, the audience finds this funny. Another laugh.

Tiffany comes to the door, and we go through our opening business, which establishes that she is prim and proper and I am a total idiot, which doesn't take much acting because it is pretty much real life anyway. But something is happening. I'm not making up lines, but I am making bigger gestures, broader moves, weirder voices than I did in rehearsal. People are howling. Tiffany's eyes are dancing, and I can see that she is trying not to laugh. I am feeling like a genius.

We get to the imaginary restaurant. Laurel comes out

to take our order, and I have the same effect on her.

I am starting to feel as if I'm having an out-of-body experience. Who is this funny person, making everyone laugh? How long can it go on? Can I keep it going, keep cranking up the jokes, hold on to this glorious lightning bolt I'm riding?

Laurel disappears to get our order. I fake blowing my nose on the cloth napkin, then inspecting it to see the results. I act as if I am fascinated by my imaginary boogers. Tiffany acts as if she is repulsed, but I can see she is hardly able to keep from bursting into laughter—especially when I hand the napkin across the table so she can examine it, too.

The audience is just about screaming. I am beginning to think that this kind of laughter is even better than the sound of Tiffany's voice.

Laurel comes back with our "order," which, because this is a skit and we are on a low budget, is a plate of Hostess cupcakes. Chocolate.

I am supposed to eat in a disgusting way. The script does not specify how. Still riding my wave of improvisation inspiration, I pick up a cupcake and stuff the entire thing into my mouth. Tiffany's eyes widen, and she turns her head to hide the laugh she can't hold in. Her shoulders are shaking. This is too good to be true.

I deliver my next line—which is about how beautiful she is—with bits of chocolate spewing out. It's disgusting but hilarious. Tiffany has tears streaming down her cheeks from trying to hold in her laughter.

Desperate to keep the riff going, I cram another entire cupcake into my mouth.

This is when disaster strikes. Suddenly, I discover that I can't breathe because there is a chocolate logjam in my throat. I only need a minute, I think, and I'll get this. I try to give my next line, but nothing comes out. Tiffany looks alarmed. The audience is still laughing, but the laughter is starting to die down, as if some of them realize I am in trouble.

Which is when Mikey comes barreling on stage from behind me, screaming, "He's choking! He's choking!" Then he grabs me around the waist and jabs his fists into my belly.

I've been Heimliched!

Those of you who know about the Heimlich maneuver will remember that basically it forces the air out of your lungs, blowing whatever is blocking your breathing out of your mouth.

Those of you who have been staging this in your mind as you read will remember who is directly across from me.

Those of you with even minimal powers of prediction will know what happens next. An unholy mix of partially chewed Hostess chocolate cupcakes spews out of my mouth and spatters all over Tiffany.

I am filled with deeper horror than any I have ever known. Wrenching my way out of Mikey's grasp, I bolt around the table to clean her off.

Unfortunately, the table is close to the edge of the stage.

Too close. Tripping over my untied shoelace, I hurtle headfirst into the darkness.

My body makes some very unpleasant sounds as it lands.

Okay, I probably could have accepted the broken leg.

I might even have been able to live with the memory of the look on Tiffany's face.

But when the ambulance guys came and put me on a stretcher, and everyone stood there watching as they rolled me out of the school, and Mikey followed after them to tell me that my fly had been open during the entire fiasco, I really thought that was too much.

Anyway, that's how I ended up in this hospital bed, staring at my right leg, which is up in traction.

Tiffany came to visit a while ago. That would have been wonderful, except she brought along her boyfriend, Chuck. He goes to another school and is old enough to drive.

Something inside me died when she introduced him.

To make things worse (and what doesn't?), it turns out that Chuck was in the audience yesterday.

"You were brilliant, man," he says. "At least, until the part where it all fell to pieces."

I want to shove a Hostess cupcake down his throat.

After they are gone, Mikey shows up.

"Tough luck, Murphy," he says, looking at my cast.

I try to remember that he is my best friend and really thought he was saving my life when he Heimliched me.

It is not easy.

"Cheer up," he says. "It couldn't get worse than this."

He's lucky my leg is in traction and I can't get out of bed. He is also lucky I don't have a cupcake on me.

After Mikey leaves, I make two decisions: (a) I am going to change my name and (b) I never want to be thirteen again as long as I live.

There is another knock on my door.

"Hello, Murphy," says a soft voice.

It's Laurel.

She smiles shyly. "Can I come in?"

I've never noticed how pretty she is when she smiles. For a brief moment I think life may not be so bad after all.

I am fairly certain, however, that this is a delusion.

After all, my name is still Murphy Murphy.

And I'm still thirteen years old.

I don't even want to think about what might happen next.

Okay, her name wasn't really Tiffany, it was Sue. But she really did sit in front of me in social studies, she really did have golden hair, and she really did ask me to be in a skit with her, though it was for a religious youth group, not our school's drama club.

As for the cupcake, it wasn't chocolate, it was one of those orange Hostess things. But I really did stuff the whole thing in my mouth (only one, thank goodness), and it really was funny when I did it.

Most of the rest of the stuff I made up.

Except for falling off the stage.

The weird thing is, I didn't even remember I had done that until after I had written the story and was talking to Jim Howe about what was real and what I had made up.

The other weird thing is, I wasn't thirteen when I fell off that stage; I was in my forties.

I don't want to scare you, but that's one of the things about being thirteen: No matter how old you get, you never quite outgrow it.

Bruce Coville

yearbook photo

Bruce Coville was born and raised in upstate New York, where he still makes his home. Growing up in the country, around the corner from his grandparents' farm, he had lots of time to read and daydream—though he also had to put in a lot of backbreaking work helping in the garden and bringing in the hay and, later, digging graves. (His grandfather was caretaker for the cemetery.)

Bruce decided to become a children's book writer when he was nineteen and suffered a mere eight years of struggle and rejection before he sold his first book. Since then he has published over eighty books for young readers, including *My Teacher Is an Alien* and *Jeremy Thatcher, Dragon Hatcher.*

In addition to his work as a writer, Bruce produces, directs, and sometimes narrates audiobooks, originally for Listening Library and now for his own company, Full Cast Audio. He has also performed his own work with the Syracuse Symphony Orchestra and Open Hand Theater, and he travels extensively to speak at schools and conferences.

Kate the Great

Meg Cabot

Okay, so my mom said that when I turned thirteen, I would finally be allowed to do the two things I'd always wanted to do:

1. Get my ears pierced
2. Babysit

Not just, you know, look out for my little brothers while my mom was at the store, either, but babysit for people not related to me. For actual money.

The ear-piercing thing was supposed to be the cinchy part. Except, of course, it wasn't, because my mom wouldn't let me just go to the mall and get my ears pierced at Claire's like Kate Malloy did. No, *my* mom had to take me to the *doctor's* office to have my ears pierced.

Even the *doctor* thought it was weird.

"Most people take their daughters to Claire's," he told my mom.

But Mom was totally inflexible. I was not going to die of blood poisoning if she had anything to say about it—even though there have been no reported deaths from blood poisoning of people who got their ears pierced at Claire's in the entire history of the mall. If I wanted my ears pierced, Dr. Bomba would have to do it, and that was the end of it.

And even though I haven't gotten blood poisoning (so far), the holes aren't even. My mom swears that isn't true, but it totally is.

Kate didn't get blood poisoning from Claire's, and her ear holes aren't uneven, either.

The babysitting thing, though. Now, *that* wasn't going to be so easy. That's because there aren't that many little kids in my neighborhood. Most of the kids who live on our street are older than me, like Kate Malloy.

But the good thing is, a new couple, the Weinmans, moved in down the street, and they adopted a Chinese baby, because they can't have a baby of their own, my mom said.

Only I wasn't supposed to mention that last part to anyone, she said.

Anyway, I wasn't especially stoked about the Weinmans' baby, since the Weinmans live right next door to Kate Malloy and I figured they'd ask her to babysit before they'd ever ask me, on account of Kate living so close by and being two years older than me and already in high school and everything.

So when my mom told me, about a week after my thirteenth birthday—my ear holes were still sort of squishy; Dr. Bomba said that I have to twist my posts every morning and night to keep the uneven holes he'd punched into my earlobes from closing up—that Mrs. Weinman had called and asked if I—me, Jenny Greenley—could babysit Saturday night . . . well, I was pretty stoked. I even went to the library and checked out a book on babysitting so I would know what to do in an emergency if Molly—that was the baby's name—started choking on her own spit-up or whatever.

I guess I didn't think much about why the Weinmans had asked me, and not Kate, to babysit for Molly. I just figured they'd called Kate and she had been busy or something. Kate was starting tenth grade in the fall. I am only going into eighth. Tenth graders have a way more active social life than eighth graders. I know this on account of movies and TV. And from Kate telling me, every day, on the way home from the bus stop.

So when I got to the Weinmans' on Saturday night, and I was standing there while Mrs. Weinman told me where everything was and gave me her cell number in case of an emergency with Molly and all, I was kind of surprised when she went, in a nervous way, "Oh, and, Jenny, I don't know whether or not you are friends with the girl next door, Kate Malloy, but I would appreciate it if you wouldn't have her over while we are gone."

What surprised me about this is:

1. It had never occurred to me to have anyone over while I was babysitting (this seemed to me like it might be a distraction from my job, which was to watch Molly); and
2. The Weinmans didn't like Kate.

According to Kate, she is one of the most popular girls in school. Everyone likes Kate.

Except Mrs. Weinman, apparently.

After the Weinmans left, I sat in the living room with a Coke—my mom never has soda in the house, on account of it causing cavities and diabetes and all of that—next to little Molly, who was dozing in her little bouncy chair, and watched TV. The Weinmans, unlike us, had all the premium cable movie channels.

I couldn't believe how great babysitting was. All I had to do was sit there and make sure Molly didn't choke to death on her own spit-up, and I could have all the Coke I wanted while watching HBO! I reached up as I sat there and twisted my gold posts. *Squish, squish.* Being thirteen *rocked.*

I had just decided this when the doorbell rang. I was kind of surprised, since the Weinmans had only just left. I thought maybe they had forgotten their keys or something.

But when I opened the front door, it wasn't either Mr. or Mrs. Weinman standing on the porch. It was Kate. Kate Malloy. Along with a boy I recognized from the bus. He was in Kate's grade and lived a few blocks away.

"I knew it," Kate said when she saw me, her pretty blue eyes narrowing. She didn't look too happy to see me. "I thought that was you. I saw you in the window as we were walking by. I should have known they'd call you instead of me."

I swallowed. This was bad. Very bad.

"Well," Kate said, "aren't you going to invite us in?"

"Um," I said. I wasn't nervous just because Mrs. Weinman had told me specifically not to have Kate over and it was my first babysitting job and I didn't want to mess up. And I wasn't nervous just because it was Kate and every time Kate saw me lately she called me a baby. No, I was also nervous because when I looked at the boy—he was tall and skinny, with very dark hair but very light blue eyes—I saw that he was holding a can with tinfoil wrapped all around it, so you couldn't see what he was drinking.

"Come on, Jen," Kate said. "Let us in."

"Mrs. Weinman doesn't want, um, people to come over while they're out," I said. I said *people* instead of *you* because I didn't want to hurt Kate's feelings.

"So?" Kate said. "What the Whine-Mans don't know won't hurt them. Don't be such a baby." Then she pushed me out of the way and came inside.

I didn't know what to do. I didn't want to act like a baby, especially in front of a boy—a high school boy. But at the same time, I didn't want to mess up my first babysitting job ever.

I looked at the boy, who was still standing on the front porch.

"Hi," he said, sticking out his hand. It was long and pale and skinny, like the rest of him. "I'm Patrick."

No boy had ever offered to shake hands with me before. I put my hand in his and shook it.

"I'm Jenny," I said, and because I couldn't help it, I looked at the tinfoil-wrapped can in his other hand.

"Oh," he said, letting go of my hand and reaching over to peel back some of the foil. "It's just Dr Pepper. The foil keeps it cold."

I saw the familiar maroon background with the white stripe and felt relieved. Then I felt embarrassed because it occurred to me that maybe Patrick thought I was a baby, like Kate was always saying, on account of me thinking there was beer in that can.

In the living room, I heard the volume on the TV go up. Way up. It woke Molly. She started to cry.

I let go of the screen door and went into the living room. Patrick followed me. Kate was standing in the middle of the room, holding the remote control and flipping through the channels, fast.

"Kate," I said, "the TV's too loud. It's upsetting Molly."

Kate looked down at Molly. "She likes it," was all she said, and went on flipping channels.

Patrick looked down at Molly, too. "I don't think she likes it," he said.

Kate threw the remote control onto the coffee table and said, "Whatever," in a bored voice. Then she collapsed onto the couch and went, "Pat and I are on our way downtown to the Penguin to get Blizzards. Come with us."

"I can't go downtown," I said, a little shocked at the suggestion. "I have to stay here with Molly."

Kate went, "The Whine-Mans left a number, right? Call them and tell them Molly is sick. Then they'll come home, and we can all go downtown."

I was even more shocked. First of all, I am not allowed to go downtown without an adult after dark. And second, it was my first-ever babysitting job, and all.

"I can't do that," I said.

"Why not?" Kate had let her baby tee hike up, so we could all her see her flat belly above the waistband of her low-ride jeans. My mom won't let me wear baby tees or low-ride pants. Kate said because of this, everyone in high school will think I am a baby.

"Because it would be lying," I said. I unbuckled Molly and picked her up from the bouncy seat, hoping that if I held her, she would stop crying. It didn't seem to work, though.

"Oh, God," Kate said with a sneer. "I forgot. Little Jenny Greenley never lies." She looked over at Patrick. "I keep telling her she's never going to make it through ninth grade. She's going to get eaten alive."

Patrick was looking at Molly, who was getting kind of red in the face. He said, "Come on, Kate. She's busy with the baby. Let's go."

But Kate didn't look ready to go. She stayed where she was on the couch. "I wonder why they asked you to babysit and not me," she said. "The Whine-Mans, I mean."

"Because they probably thought you were busy," I said. I didn't want to tell Kate about Mrs. Weinman not liking her. Because even though Kate is always hurting my feelings, I didn't want to hurt hers. "With you being in high school, and all."

"Yeah," Kate said. "But I have more experience with babies. You would think they would want the best care possible for their kid, instead of bringing in some neophyte."

Kate does that a lot. Uses words she knows I won't understand because I'm not in high school yet.

"Look," I said. I didn't want to, because I was afraid she might make fun of me some more in front of Patrick. But Molly was still crying, and I needed to calm her down, and I didn't think I could do that with Kate and a strange boy in the house. "You guys just go on downtown and have Blizzards without me. I'll come some other time."

Kate sat up. "You know what that baby probably needs? Some music. Babies like music."

Kate picked up the remote control and turned the channel to MTV. But the music they play on MTV is not really the kind of music babies like. It just made Molly cry harder.

"I think she needs some quiet time!" I yelled, starting to feel desperate.

"She's just hungry," Kate said. I was blocking her view of the TV, and she had to lean over to see around me. "Give her a bottle, and she'll be all right."

"No," I said. "I think—"

Kate looked mad, and not just about me blocking her view. "God," Kate said, "she's just hungry. I know, I have brothers and sisters, remember? Or maybe you don't remember, because you haven't been over to my house in so long. Always busy with your new friends, aren't you, Jen?"

I stood there holding Molly as she screamed in my ear. It was true. I *hadn't* been over to Kate's house in a long time. I used to go over there every single day. In spite of the difference in our ages, Kate and I had been best friends once. We'd done everything together: gone to the pool and to the library every day all summer; sat in the back of the bus, where it was bumpiest, to and from school; spent the night at each other's houses . . . everything. We had been inseparable. I had thought Kate was the coolest person in the world. I was always copying her, reading the books she read, trying to get my mom to get me the clothes she wore. When Kate had begun calling herself "Kate the Great," after we'd read a book about King Arthur and the knights of the Round Table, I had made up a name for myself: "Jenny the Intrepid." It didn't sound as good as Kate the Great, but there aren't many words that rhyme with Jenny.

And then last year Kate had gone to the high school, leaving me behind in seventh grade. And suddenly, she didn't want to go to the library anymore. She wanted to go to the mall. When we went to the pool, she didn't actually want to get in the water; she wanted to lie around in her bikini and work on her tan. These things were kind of boring to me. Whenever I tried to remind her about being Kate the Great and Jenny the Intrepid, she told me not to be so babyish. She started telling me how I was never going to fit in when I got to high school. Like how, in high school, if you don't blow-dry your hair straight or have nice clothes, no one will speak to you.

This hurt my feelings, of course, but there was nothing I could do about it. My mom told me that sometimes people just grow apart and that I should try to make some new friends. Eventually, I did. Making friends, it turns out, is easy, once you get over being shy. All you have to do is go up to a person who you know is nice and talk to her about stuff you know she likes. Then she will be your friend.

I got a lot of new friends. But then, so had Kate.

I reminded her of this by saying, with a glance in Patrick's direction, "You have new friends, too."

"Yeah," Kate said. "But I don't get why you'd rather be hanging out with your little baby friends when you could be hanging out with me. I mean, don't you think hanging with someone in high school would be more fun than hanging with some eighth grader?"

It made me mad when she said that. I mean, *she* was the one who'd forgotten all about being Kate the Great and Jenny the Intrepid. *She*'s the one who was always going around telling me I'm such a baby.

My being mad at Kate gave me the courage to say to her, "Look, I'm sorry, but you have to leave now."

Kate didn't like hearing that very much.

"What?" she said with an incredulous laugh.

"You have to leave now," I said again. This time, I didn't say it with as much conviction because the look on Kate's face was scaring me. But I still said it. And as I said it, I leaned down and, holding Molly with one arm, snatched the remote control away from Kate.

Then I turned the TV off.

Kate's face got almost as red as Molly's when I did that. But not because she was embarrassed. Because she was mad.

"You know, Jen," she said in a very hard voice, "you should really try to be a little more grateful that I am even willing to hang out with you. I mean, I have a lot better things to do than hang around a whiny little eighth grader."

I was tired of her always reminding me about what a baby I am. I went, "If you have so many better things to do than hang around with me, why don't you go do them, then? I don't even *like* you anymore, Kate. All you ever do is call me names and tell me how babyish I am. If that's what you think of me, why don't you just go away and leave me *alone*?"

Even as the words were coming out of my mouth, I couldn't believe I was saying them. I mean, this was *Kate* I was talking to. We had shared bowls of cake frosting with each other. We had made capes for ourselves out of towels and pretended our bikes were horses and played Kate the Great and Jenny the Intrepid, knights of the Round Table.

And now Jenny the Intrepid was telling Kate the Great to leave her alone.

Kate's face went as white beneath her tan as if I had slapped her. Then she said—not yelling at all, which was somehow scarier than if she'd really let loose—"Fine. If that's how you feel, Jenny. Only don't expect me to come to your rescue when you start high school and no one will talk to you because you are such an immature freak. I mean, when the girls in the bathroom see you come in, with your stupid Tretorns and classic-cut jeans, and they knock you down and start trying to put their cigarettes out in your notebooks, don't think *I'm* going to help you out."

"I don't *want* your help," I assured her.

"Fine," Kate said. Then she spun around and started walking out of the house. "Come on, Pat."

I didn't even watch them go. Instead, I tried to comfort Molly, who was still crying. I knew how she felt. I wanted to cry, too. . . .

Especially when, after, like, ten minutes, Molly was *still* crying. I couldn't believe it. I didn't think anyone could cry for that long. I held the screaming baby, bouncing her a little in my arms, not certain what to do. Molly's face was red, and her skin felt very hot. What if she was sick or something? I thought about calling my mom and asking her to come over. But I was sure Kate would find out somehow and think I was a bigger baby than ever—you know, calling my mommy to come and take care of my problems for me.

So instead, I did what it had said to do in the babysitting book I had read. I went to the phone and dialed Mrs. Weinman's cell number.

I didn't even have to say anything. I just went, "Mrs. Weinman—"

I guess she could hear Molly's screams in the background, since she went, "We'll be home in five minutes," and hung up.

Molly didn't stop crying until Mrs. Weinman, looking as scared as the mom from *Poltergeist* when she's trying to keep Carol Ann from going into the light, came in and took her from me and went, "There, there. It's all right," to the baby. "Everything is going to be all right."

Mr. Weinman stood in the doorway, gazing worriedly at his wife and daughter.

"What happened?" he wanted to know.

"I don't know," I said. "She just wouldn't stop crying." I didn't mention the part about Kate coming over.

"She's all right," Mrs. Weinman said, kissing Molly on the forehead. And Molly did look a lot better already. Her face was back to a normal color, and she was only crying very softly now. "She just needed her mommy. Didn't you, Molly? I'm going to try to put her to bed. It's all right, Jenny. You can go on home."

I felt really bad. I said, "Oh, no. You guys go ahead and go back out. I just thought she was sick or something. Now that she's really all right, I can stay."

"No," Mrs. Weinman said. "You go on home. I don't think Molly's ready for babysitters yet."

What she really meant was that *I* wasn't ready for babysitting yet. She didn't say so, but I knew that was what she was thinking. I wondered if the Weinmans would ever ask me to babysit again. I kind of doubted it.

I really doubted it when Mr. Weinman picked up Patrick's foil-wrapped Dr Pepper, which he'd left sitting on the coffee table, and asked me, "Is this yours, Jenny?"

"No," I said. Then, realizing what I'd done, I went, "I mean, yes."

Mrs. Weinman looked at me curiously from the doorway. She said, "Jenny, you didn't by any chance have visitors over here while we were gone, did you?"

I said, turning bright red from my forehead to my earring holes, "Of course not."

I'm not sure either of them believed me. All I know is, I couldn't look the Weinmans in the eye as I said, "I'm glad Molly's all right. I'm sorry if your evening got screwed up. Good-bye."

I managed to make it out of their house before the tears came. I cried the whole way home—not far, since the Weinmans only live a few doors down from me. I couldn't believe what an idiot I had been. I didn't know how I was going to face my mother, who'd wonder what I was doing home so early. I'd have to tell her the truth—at least the part about thinking Molly was sick—because she'd be sure to talk to Mrs. Weinman tomorrow.

I went up to my front porch and sat down on the top step, lowered my forehead to my knees, and sobbed. I didn't care who heard me, or who saw me, even. I was too mad to care.

The worst part of it was that it wasn't even Kate's fault that the Weinmans would never ask me to babysit again. It was *my* fault, for not having stood up to her in the first place. I should have told her a long time ago what I thought of her, and her always telling me what a baby I was. I *had* been a baby ever to have let her treat me the way she had.

I don't know how long I sat there crying. I stopped when a mosquito bit me and I had to lift up my head to see where it was so I could smack it. I missed, though.

Then I saw some feet come out of the dark grass of the lawn and into the circle of light thrown by the porch lamp. To my surprise, Kate's friend Patrick was standing there. He said, "Hey. Are you okay?"

"Yeah," I said, red-faced that he had almost caught me crying. "I guess."

"Oh," he said. In the porch light, he looked as embarrassed as I felt. "Good. I just was on my way home and saw you. . . ."

Heard me, was more like it. I reached up and wiped away what was left of my tears.

"I'm fine," I said, trying to mean it. "Why aren't you downtown with Kate, getting Blizzards?"

"Oh." Patrick looked uncomfortable. "Well, I guess I kind of blew her off. She makes me so mad sometimes. You know?"

Did I ever.

"That was really uncool of her, what she did to you,

with the baby and all," he went on. "And all that stuff she said about high school. You know, about girls lighting your notebooks on fire if you wear the wrong shoes."

I swallowed. "Yeah," I said.

"It's not true," he said.

"Really?" I was kind of shocked by this. "Then . . . why did she say it?"

"I don't know." Patrick sat down on the cement step beneath mine and looked out at our lawn. Lightning bugs were flying around, blinking on and off, like when my little brothers played disco with the light switch in the basement. "I think she wanted to make sure you'd stay friends with her. You know, by making you think you needed her to help you get through ninth grade in another year. Kate doesn't have many friends."

"She doesn't?" This surprised me. About Kate not having many friends, I mean. "She's always going on about how popular she is and how many parties she gets invited to and all the people who like her and stuff."

"Well," Patrick said, "she's not. Popular, I mean. I think she just tells you that stuff to make herself sound . . . you know. Cool. And important."

I looked at him. It was pretty weird, to be sitting there on my front porch, talking to a boy, especially one who was so much older than me—two whole years—and in high school and everything.

Still, in spite of the weirdness—maybe because of my newfound intrepidness or something—I heard myself asking, "Why do *you* hang around with her?"

"I don't know," he said, swatting at a mosquito. "I guess I feel kind of sorry for her."

"Oh," I said.

And just like that, I stopped hating Kate. Not that I was going to rush out and be her friend again or anything. It was just . . . well, in spite of what she'd done to me, making me lose my first babysitting job and all, I realized that her life was way worse than mine. Because at least I don't have to go around lying about how popular I am. And at least I don't have boys hanging out with me because they feel sorry for me.

"Well," Patrick said, standing up again, "I better go. Sorry about that whole thing with the baby. I hope we didn't get you into trouble."

"That's okay," I said, smiling. Because, suddenly, it was.

"See you in school," he said, and started to walk away.

"Oh," I said. "But I don't go to your school."

He looked back at me. "You will," he said. "And I'll see you then."

Then he walked out of the ring of porch light and into the darkness.

I reached up and twisted my earrings, the way Dr. Bomba had told me to. *Squish, squish.* Then I went inside.

I hated being thirteen. I felt like an adult, but on the few occasions when someone was prepared to treat me like one, I screwed it up somehow! "Kate the Great" is based on an incident that really did happen to me. It is also about two girls who were once best friends but are slowly growing apart—something that also seemed to happen a lot as I got older.

P.S. The Weinmans (names have been changed to protect the innocent) never asked me to babysit again!

Meg Cabot

Meg Cabot was born and raised in Bloomington, Indiana. She moved to New York City after graduating from Indiana University and has lived there ever since. She is best known as the author of *All American Girl*, The Mediator series, and The Princess Diaries series, although she also writes books for adults. She lives with her husband and a one-eyed cat named Henrietta. You can visit her anytime you want to at www.megcabot.com.

If You Kiss a Boy

Alex Sanchez

Monday afternoon, since it's a holiday, my best friend Jamal and I walk to the mall. He's all mopey because his cool FBI baseball cap that he actually got in Washington flew out the bus window. We used to always make jokes about what the cap initials stood for, things like "Fart and Booger Instigator," dumb stuff like that.

I met Jamal when my family moved to the U.S. six years ago, when I was in second grade. He was the closest neighbor kid my age and the only boy in class who didn't pick on me because I was Mexican. He helped me practice English and taught me all the dirty words you need so you'll know what other kids are saying.

Ever since, Jamal and I always hang together. When I have to go with my parents to visit relatives in Mexico every Christmas, I beg them to let Jamal come with us, but my dad says no, he doesn't want that responsibility. I tell Dad *I'll* be responsible for Jamal, but Dad won't listen. Sometimes I wonder if it's because Jamal's black. Dad can be kind of bigoted.

At the mall, Jamal and I walk from store to store, checking out caps, but only find ones with sports teams or cities on them. That's so unoriginal. So we end up at the pet shop, which is our favorite place anyway. Okay, I'm going to tell you something only Jamal knows. I love the smell—you know, that dog-biscuit-and-hamster-shavings smell? And I love the noise—aquariums humming, birds chirping, pups yapping and barking, rattling their cages.

Jamal is all into pups. Like, I think he must've been a chocolate Labrador in a past life. Since we go to the pet shop every single time we're at the mall, the nice Asian lady owner lets Jamal play with the pups.

Today he plays with a Lab, hugging and petting her almost to death. The pup's stumpy tail wags like crazy. Joking, I warn Jamal she's going to pee on him. That actually happened once. It was kind of gross but funny.

Jamal just laughs, letting the Lab pup lick his face. He has a huge blazing bright smile—Jamal, I mean. His tall lips and dark skin make his grin seem even larger. I wish I had lips like his. Mine are sort of thin and puny.

Seeing Jamal so happy makes me want to get him a pup. I would, except he lives in an apartment complex that doesn't allow dogs, only fish and cats. That's funny because I'm more of a cat person, but I can't have a cat because my dad's allergic to them. "In life we always want what we can't have." That's what my mom says.

After the pet shop we go to the food court and get french fries. It's a good thing they don't charge for ketchup because Jamal slathers his potatoes like a madman.

Since today's a holiday, the food court is jam-packed. About a million cell phones go off. Each time, people fumble around to see if it's theirs.

Because Jamal and I don't have one, we do this thing where every time a cell rings, we grope our pockets or grab whatever, pretending it's our phone. Today when one rings, Jamal grabs the plastic saltshaker and starts talking into it. Then another phone rings, so I think fast and grab this really long skinny potato, dangling it around my ear like a hands-free mike. All these people walk by staring. It's awesome.

After eating, we check out the multiplex. A movie about a time machine is about to start, but I don't have enough money.

"I'll pay," Jamal says, pulling out his wallet.

"But what about getting your cap?"

Jamal makes a face. "They all suck."

He and I are always lending each other money anyway. Not really lending, since we don't actually keep track. We figure it evens out. I give him all the money I have, and he uses it toward popcorn and Cokes.

The theater's empty except for a guy and lady couple. We sit on the aisle, where Jamal likes to sit, and kick our legs over the seats in front of us. The movie totally sucks.

By the looks of the poster outside, the film's supposed to be an adventure, but instead it's this stupid romance, where some buff guy time travels to Victorian New York, where he falls in love with a bimbo babe and they say crap like, "It's the first time I've ever felt this way."

It's sooo bad, the guy and lady walk out. Jamal and I would, too, except now we have the whole place to ourselves. So we start shouting our own dialogue lines for the actors. Dumb stuff, like the babe telling the guy, "Excuse me while I fart."

Jamal laughs so hard, he leans over, nearly choking on his popcorn. I'm laughing, too, and pat him on the back, which only makes him laugh harder. So then I reach over and grab him round the waist like I'm doing the Heimlich maneuver, even though I don't really know how. That makes him crack up even more. Next thing I know, we're stumbling into the aisle and onto the carpet, rolling on top of each other.

We're both the same size, and he's lying on top of me, his body shaking with laughter. My arms surround him, still trying my own version of the Heimlich, except he's facing me, laughing, wheezing, and saying, "It's the first time I've ever felt this way."

His weight presses warm against me, his face leaning close, his popcorn breath blowing onto my cheek. I think of him hugging that pup in the store and his big happy smile. That's when it happens.

I kiss him.

It's the first time in my life kissing anyone on the mouth. At first we both keep laughing, his lips bouncing on mine, kissing me back, his breath tasting Coke-sweet. Neither of us stops to think what we're doing. All I know is, his lips feel soft and tender, and it feels good to hold him close to me. My heart thumps against my chest like that puppy's tail.

But Jamal stops laughing, and my heart flips in panic. What just happened?

He pushes off me, out of my arms, while I scramble away, embarrassed, pressing my back against the cold metal seat sides. Across the dark aisle, we each cower. My heart pounds louder than the movie sound track. From the light cast by the screen, I can see Jamal's face scrunched up. He's staring at me, his lips pressed together tight.

Even though there's no one to hear us, Jamal whispers, "Why did you do that?" His voice is tense and somber.

I try to think of an answer but can't concentrate. Too many thoughts pop in my mind. "I don't know," I tell him, though I know that's not true.

I've had these weird feelings before, thoughts I've heard are wrong. I've tried to push them deep down inside me. Till now.

"Are you mad at me?" I ask.

His face is blank, his eyes like deep wells. "I don't know," he says, eyeing me like he's thinking.

"I'm sorry," I tell him and swallow hard, my heart racing—but not like a pup's tail, more like horse hooves wanting to gallop away.

"We better go," he says.

In the light of the lobby, my eyes hurt. I lift my hand to shield them as we walk home together, silent and sullen. No dumb jokes now. It's like suddenly there's a wall between us.

What have I done? He's my best friend. How could I do that? I want to go back in time, erase it. But when I glance over at him, all I can think is how good it felt.

What's wrong with me? How can I think that? I keep a little behind him, not wanting him to look at me and wishing he would.

When we get to the street where our paths separate, Jamal stops. He keeps his gaze on the sidewalk, biting his lip. His face is still scrunched up, his sixteen brown freckles (I've counted) even darker than his skin.

"I'm going home now," he mumbles toward the sidewalk, but he doesn't move.

I want to say something and try to talk about what we did, tell him how I feel. Except I'm not sure how I feel. I have so many different feelings that I can't sort out the words.

He glances up at me, his lip quivering, like he's confused, too. "See you later," he says.

"See you," I respond softly as he turns away. I want to stop him. I want to hug him. Instead, I watch him walk away down the street.

I want to run after him. I want to bolt home. I wish he'd turn around and come back. But he just disappears around the corner.

I walk home thinking, thinking, thinking. In my room, I immediately turn on the TV. But even though I sit in bed, right in front of the tube with the sound blaring at me, I'm not watching. I'm inside my head kissing Jamal and wondering, Why on earth did I do it?

I pick up the remote control and turn the volume higher.

Mom comes to the door and tells me, "*Por favor, mi amor,* turn it down. Wash up for dinner."

As I press the volume, something really weird happens. An ad comes on TV for *Will & Grace*—you know, that sitcom about a gay guy and his friends?

I've never actually known anyone gay. In fifth grade there was a boy who everyone said was gay because he always wanted to play with the girls. I remember being curious about him, but seeing the way other kids picked on him, I stayed away. I didn't want people thinking *I* was gay. In our school, being gay is the worst thing in the world you can be.

You hear it about a million times a day: "That's so gay." "He's so gay." "That movie was so gay." "That french fry is sooo gay." . . . Except in Mr. Bonita's class.

He's my science teacher. Everyone says he's gay, mostly because he always dresses really nice and also because of what happened one day in class, when we were supposed to be researching volcanoes.

Mr. Bonita walked around the room, helping in a hushed voice. Meanwhile, this blond boy named Curt and another boy were cracking up over some pictures in *National Geographic*.

My mom says Curt is *chusma*. That means, like, "riffraff" in Spanish.

The other boy said something I couldn't hear, but in response Curt boxed him on the shoulder and said, "You faggot!"

Mr. Bonita slammed his hand down on a desktop. "Curt!"

Twenty-three heads bobbed up in surprise, most with mouths agape. It was the first time we'd heard Mr. Bonita yell. His face was angry red.

"That's very offensive," he said, bearing down on Curt.

Students turned to each other with puzzled looks. No teacher had ever stopped us from saying *faggot* before.

"I was only kidding," Curt protested. "I didn't mean anything by it."

"You know where that word comes from?" Mr. Bonita asked.

One of the brainier girls proudly raised her hand. "It's a pile of sticks."

"That's right," Mr. Bonita said. "It comes from the bundles of wood used during the Middle Ages to burn people for being gay. It's as hateful as any racial slur. I won't tolerate it."

Mr. Bonita scanned the class. "Is that clear to everyone? I don't want to hear *faggot* or *fag* or *queer* or *homo* or even *gay* used as a put-down. If I do, you'll be reprimanded, same as for any other slur. Can everyone abide by that?"

Of course we all said yes, seeing him so angry.

Later, as we pulled our coats on to walk home, Curt leaned toward me and whispered, so close that his breath brushed my ear, "I bet you anything *he's* gay."

I bit into my lip, wanting to argue, but given Mr. Bonita's outburst, what could I say? Why would any guy speak out like that, unless he *was* gay?

Now I turn off the TV and go to the kitchen. Beside the stove, Mom pours two handfuls of rice into a pot of boiling water. She never measures anything, but it always comes out great. "Can you set the table?" she asks and adds: "How was the mall?"

I reply, "Fine," and casually ask, "Do you know anyone who's gay?"

Though I keep my eyes trained on the silverware, I can tell she's peering at me, her brow raised in question. *"Sí,"* she says. *"Por qué?"*

"Just asking," I tell her, trying not to sound too curious. In reality, my mind ricochets from one question to the other: Who is it? Anyone I know? Does Mom think they're okay, or does she think they're bad?

I start sorting the silverware and ask, "How do you know they're gay?"

"Oh . . ." She laughs the same way kids at school laugh at gay jokes. "You can tell." I laugh along with her, though it's mostly because I'm nervous.

Opening the cupboard for plates, I ask, "What makes someone gay?"

"I don't know," she says, stirring the rice. "I don't think anyone knows."

"Do you think they're bad?" I ask.

"No." Her mouth droops like she's sad. "I feel sorry for them. They have such hard lives."

That makes me recall the kid in fifth grade again. I'm thinking about that when suddenly, out of nowhere, Mom asks, "Did you and Jamal have a fight?"

It's kind of weird how she can always tell when something's wrong.

Her fingertips reach out, gently brushing the hair from my forehead. Her hand smells like rice. I want to tell her what happened, but what would I say? I can't tell her Jamal and I kissed.

Instead, I shake my head and carry the plates and silver to the dining room, trying not to drop them.

Later, at dinner, even though I'm starving, I can't eat. My stomach is as tight as a fist. All I can think about is, what if Jamal tells his mom what we did and then she calls and tells my mom and dad?

I try to reassure myself: Jamal won't tell anyone. If he did, he'd be admitting he did it, too. After all, he kissed me back. And he didn't pull away, at least not at first. It was like he wanted to do it. He could've stopped me.

The phone rings. I jump in my seat. My dad gets up to answer. I stare at the uneaten chicken on my plate, sweat trickling down my forehead.

Dad grabs the receiver. "Hello?"

I hold my breath, listening.

It's my aunt from Veracruz. Relieved, I let out my breath.

While Dad talks to Aunt Dolores, I realize Mom is staring at me. "You haven't eaten anything," she says.

"I'm not hungry," I tell her, even though I'm about to faint from starvation.

After she and Dad finish eating, I help clear the table. Mom saves my meal plate. "In case you get hungry later."

After dinner, Dad asks me to help him install some

new software. He's not very good with computers. I don't mind. At least it takes my mind off the whole Jamal thing.

While we're waiting for the product download, Dad asks, "How's school going?" That's what he always asks.

And, as always, I say, "Fine."

We keep waiting for the stupid download, which takes forever. By now I'm thinking about Jamal again. "Dad, can I ask you a question?"

"Of course," he says. "What is it?"

My hands feel sticky with sweat. I try to think how to ask what I want to say. "Um . . . it's about . . ." I wipe my hands on my pants. "Somebody at school says someone is gay."

"Come on, son," Dad tells me. "You know kids say things like that all the time. Just ignore it."

"But . . ." I wipe my hands again. "Suppose it's true—do you think it's wrong?"

His gaze moves across my face, studying me, making me wish I hadn't said anything.

"I think," Dad finally says, "it's an illness. People like that are sick."

My heart sinks. I know he doesn't mean sick-sick. He means pervie-sick. It's what everyone at school says. But Will on TV doesn't act like a perv. And Mr. Bonita, if he *is* gay, doesn't either. He's one of the best teachers I've ever had.

Thank God the download finally completes. I finish the installation, and Dad pats me on the back. He used to kiss me good night on the cheek, and I'd kiss him back. No one ever said that was pervie. So why is it so pervie to kiss another guy? Who decides this stuff, anyway?

"Good night," I tell Dad and head to the kitchen to try another crack at dinner. My stomach is gurgling and groaning.

Mom's on the phone, gabbing with her friend Rosa, and I get this wild thought: Maybe I should call Mr. Bonita, tell him what happened.

But then I think: Yeah, right. Like I'd have the nerve to do that.

Mom smiles when I start picking at my dinner. But I can barely swallow. I only manage to get half the meal down before I go to my room.

Lying down in bed, I cross my arms and stare up at the ceiling. I think about Jamal, lying on top of me, on the carpeted aisle of the theater.

It wasn't the first time I've held him. We've always wrestled and tickled each other to death. I used to swipe his FBI cap off his head and bolt down the street with him chasing me.

Since his legs are longer than mine, he'd always end up catching me and pinning me down. It felt so good to feel him close to me. I'd feel more alive and electric than ever in my life, even though I nearly died from being tickled.

Finally, I'd say, "I give up," and he'd let go of me.

I'd stand, pretending to be sorry. But as soon as he wasn't looking, I'd swipe his cap again, and we'd start over.

I don't get it. How can something that felt so good be so bad?

Through my bedroom window, a sliver of new moon hangs like a fingernail against the sky. I wonder what Jamal is thinking right now. Maybe I should call him.

We've always talked about everything, stuff I couldn't talk to my parents about. I want so badly to talk to him. But what if he's angry? What if he hates me? What if he never wants to speak to me ever again?

My nose begins to run, my throat chokes up, and I know I'm about to cry.

The next morning, I wake up so hungry my stomach hurts. As I sit up, the memory of the day before comes back like a bad dream, making me return beneath the covers. What if Jamal tells the other boys at school?

"*Qué te pasa?*" Mom says, marching in to rouse me. "You're going to be late."

"I don't feel well," I mumble.

Her brow arches into a question mark. Bringing the thermometer from the medicine cabinet, she takes my temperature. While she's doing that, her hands press the glands on my throat. Next she asks, "Have you gone to the bathroom?"

Ugh, I hate when she asks that. It makes me feel like a snotty kid. "Yes," I protest.

She studies me, pouting. "Is something bothering you?"

I want to say yes. I want to tell her everything. I want to beg her not to make me go to school. But I don't. I can't. Instead, I shake my head. "No."

"Then get dressed," she tells me, and I know from her tone that she means it.

Because I took so long to get up, it's too late to walk. So Dad has to drive me.

"What's the matter?" he grumbles. "Mom says you're not feeling well."

I must look pretty wrecked, because he reaches across the seat and pats my shoulder. "You okay?"

I wish I could tell him what's the matter and curl into his arms, like when I was little. But I can't even look at him right now because I know I'll start crying again. So I just mumble, "I'm all right," unable to tell him I'm a perv.

The front of school is packed with kids. I look toward the balustrade by the steps, where Jamal and I meet every morning and after school. I'll reach out for his hand, and we'll do this combination handshake thing that only he and I do. It's kind of too complicated to describe how we press our thumbs together and wrap our pinkies.

But today he's not by the balustrade. Is he avoiding me?

Slowly, I walk down the hall toward homeroom. Locker doors slam. Kids laugh and play-punch. And of course, every few steps, someone says, "That's so gay."

Maybe I should just leave—you know, skip. Curt does it all the time. Jamal and I were going to skip one day last spring and go to the aquarium downtown. We had it all planned, but then we chickened out—the same as I do now.

At the hallway's end, I turn the corner and my stomach

drops. Jamal is at his locker, talking to Curt. Immediately, I think: He's telling Curt about me.

I edge back, wanting to run away, but Curt turns and sees me. I expect him to sneer at me, cuss me out like I've seen him yell at other people.

But he merely cracks his crazy half grin and says, "Hey."

"Hey," I respond. I glance at Jamal.

He doesn't turn to me, though, and doesn't say hi. He's mad—or confused. I know because that's what he does when he gets that way—he ignores me.

Like the time I forgot about the dog show, even though we'd planned it for months, or the time when I got that Confederate flag belt buckle without realizing it's offensive to black people.

Well, at least it seems he hasn't said anything to Curt. Still, it hurts to be ignored. I wish he'd just yell at me and get it over with. Instead, I'm left wondering: What will happen? Something's got to happen.

All during classes, I keep expecting the loudspeaker to crackle on and the principal to call me down to her office. Jamal, his parents, and mine will be there, waiting. Jamal will tell them what I did. Officer Gustaff will take me to juvie detention hall, where psychiatrists will confirm I'm sick in the head.

In the hall between classes, I keep expecting classmates to point and sneer at me. I feel guilty each time a friend smiles and says, "What's up?"

I say, "Nothing's up," cool as I can. But inside my head I feel like a criminal—like I have a secret they don't know.

All morning, I've dreaded lunch. I can remember when I first got to grade school and didn't have anyone to sit with, until Jamal invited me to sit with him. Not a day has passed since, unless he was sick, that we haven't sat together. Will he even want to sit with me now?

Slowly, I step toward my group's table. Jamal sits at the end. Even though he doesn't look up at me, I'm sure he sees me. I decide to sit at the other end.

Between us sit Curt and some other boys, talking about sex, as usual. Ever since seventh grade, it's the only thing they talk about, qualifying any female, even remotely human, as a babe.

Last week Curt got caught French-kissing beneath the gym bleachers. The girl hasn't come back to school since, probably because she's so embarrassed. But Curt brags about it every day, as if he's God's gift to babedom.

I sit silently, picking at my fish sticks and mashed potatoes. The mere thought of putting my tongue in a girl's mouth ties my stomach in knots. Before, I always thought I was just a late bloomer. But after what happened with Jamal, I wonder if that's really it.

After listening for way too long, I finally ask, "Can't we talk about something else?"

"What's the matter?" Curt grins. "Don't you like girls? You a homo?"

I cringe, immediately hoping no one saw it. "No!" I snap back at Curt. "I'm just not a sex maniac like you."

I hope that'll shut him up. But instead, he says, "I know," and smiles even wider.

The other boys laugh—everyone except Jamal. For the first time today, he makes eye contact with me, at least for a sec. I so badly wish I knew what he's thinking.

In the afternoon I have art with Ms. Dixon, then English with Ms. Jeffries. Last period is science with Mr. Bonita. As he walks around class asking questions, I find myself watching him, trying to detect some sign of . . . I don't know . . . something to tell me if he really is gay. He doesn't look it. Of course, neither does Will on TV.

Plus there's another thing: Mr. Bonita wears a gold ring on the third finger of his left hand. What the heck does that mean?

And if Mr. Bonita is gay, why's he hiding it? Why hasn't he come out and told us? It all kind of makes me angry.

Even though I know the answers to the questions he's asking, I refuse to raise my hand.

Mr. Bonita looks over at me, like he's curious why I'm not saying anything. When the final bell rings, I quickly stuff my books into my backpack.

"Joe?" Mr. Bonita says. "Can you stay for a minute?"

Curt, who always makes fun of Mr. Bonita, smirks at me, making a kiss-kiss face. I don't know why I'm even friends with Curt. Sometimes I want to smack him, even if he is bigger than me.

As the other kids clear out, Mr. Bonita sits down in the desk next to me. "Is everything okay?"

I keep my gaze lowered, wishing I could tell him everything, wishing I could just ask him if he's gay. But what if he isn't? Worse yet, what if he *is*? What would I say *then*?

"You seem upset," he tells me.

I shrug, totally wanting to talk, but I can't. My throat feels like a desert, while my eyes are turning into lakes. I know if I stay any longer, I'm going to burst out crying. I swallow hard and say, "I need to go."

"Okay." He gives a sigh. "You know I'm here whenever you want to talk."

I book from the room, relieved, but only for a moment.

Amid the crowd in the hall, Curt and some other boys horse around, tossing their books into their lockers. Beside them, Jamal loads his backpack.

Curt sees me and gives me one of his evil grins. "Miss Bonita didn't try anything with you, did she?"

"That's not funny," I respond and walk to my locker, trying to ignore him, though I sooo want to slug him.

Curt slams his locker and follows me, talking in a high voice, trying to imitate a girl, even though he doesn't sound anything like a girl. "Can I see you after class for a minute?" he says and starts tickling my neck.

"Cut it out," I warn him, pulling away.

"You sure?" Curt says. "I hear you like it."

I wince, immediately thinking: Jamal told him about me. My head burns with shame. I glance at Jamal, but he keeps his eyes fixed on the tile floor.

The other boys stare at me, as if waiting for me to deny what Curt said, defend myself, say something.

"Take it back," I tell Curt.

"You know it's true," he snarls. "You're as gay as he is."

He pushes me, hard, nearly knocking me off my feet.

After that, I'm not sure what happens. I guess I swing out at him, though I don't mean to. But next thing I know, my fist smacks his face. His nose gushes out blood. Kids scream, but I keep swinging.

From behind me, Mr. Bonita shouts, "Stop it!"

My feet fly off the ground as I'm yanked into the air. I keep swinging, too crazed to stop.

Mr. Bonita's hand tugs my shirt collar. "Joe!" he yells. "Stop it!" He wraps his arm around my chest, pinning my arms flat. "Calm down," he orders.

I'm still breathing hard as Mr. Bonita lets go of me. My chest rises and falls, and I think: What have I done? Never in my life have I ever hit anyone before.

"Tilt your head back," he instructs Curt.

The blood drips off Curt's chin, splattering his shirt in dark red streaks. Mr. Bonita places his fingers behind Curt's nose. "Put your fingers like this."

He asks Ms. Dixon to call the school nurse, then he turns back to Curt and me. "What happened?"

Neither Curt nor I say anything. Mr. Bonita turns to the kids looking on. "Who can tell me what happened?"

The crowd remains silent until Jamal speaks. "Curt said you and Joe were gay."

Titters of nervous laughter ring through the crowd. I wish I could disappear.

"Everyone be quiet!" Mr. Bonita yells. He turns to Curt. "What did I say about name-calling?"

Curt's brow furrows angrily as he brings his hand, crimson with blood, down from his nose. "Not to do it."

Jamal continues: "Then Curt pushed him."

"I did not," Curt protests.

Mr. Bonita scans the other kids' faces. One by one they nod, agreeing with Jamal. At the same time, Ms. Dixon rustles through the crowd with the nurse, who examines Curt's nose. "Just a bruise," she announces.

I'm glad he's not really hurt, though a part of me wishes he was.

"Okay," Mr. Bonita tells the crowd, "get to your buses. Curt and Joe, come with me."

As he walks us to the principal's, I think how every day seems to bring some new thing I can't believe I did.

In the principal's office, Curt and I each have to tell our side of what happened. Curt gets a week's suspension for starting the fight. I get a week of after-school detention for punching him in return.

Great, now *everyone* will make jokes about me staying after school with Mr. Bonita.

Curt gets to leave after talking to the principal, but Mr. Bonita says he wants to talk to me. When we get back to his room, he asks me to sit down across from him.

At first he doesn't say anything, just scratches the side of his face like he does in class when someone asks him a question that he has to think about.

"Joe," he tells me, with that tone of voice that says, *Time for the lecture.* "Just because Curt pushed you doesn't make it right for you to have punched him. You know that, don't you?"

"Yeah," I mumble, though I also know that if Curt did it again, I'd do the same thing.

While Mr. Bonita says something about escalating violence, I glance at the ring on his finger, the one I've wondered about. When he pauses, I ask, "Is that a wedding band?"

At first he doesn't answer, just studies me. Then he says, "I have a partner."

I know from watching *Will & Grace* that he doesn't mean a business partner. He means, like, a guy partner. He *is* gay.

My heart ka-thumps at the realization. I shift my feet, wanting to run, except, like, I'm glued-to-the-seat curious, too.

"My dad thinks being gay is a sickness," I tell him.

Only after I say it do I realize how mean that sounds, but it doesn't seem to bother Mr. Bonita.

"There's absolutely no scientific evidence of that," he says.

"Oh," I say. There's a question I want to ask him, but I can't. Instead, I say, "You don't think it's bad?" I realize that's kind of a stupid question, since if he thought being gay was bad, he wouldn't be gay.

"I don't think it is," he tells me.

I squirm in my seat, still unable to ask the question I most want to ask. So I say, "How did you first know you were?"

"Well . . ." He eyes me up and down, and I swear he can tell what I really want to ask. "When I watched a movie or

TV, and the guy kissed the girl, I wished the guy was kissing me."

I think back to the movie Jamal and I saw yesterday, and I wonder if that's why I kissed him.

The more Mr. Bonita talks, the more I want to ask my question. Finally, I decide I have to ask it, before my heart explodes all over the place. "Do you think . . ." I take a deep breath, feeling like I'm going to faint. ". . . I . . . am?"

I glance down, certain I must be as red as an apple. No way can I look up at him or I'm sure I'll die. In fact, I wish he'd say something quick, before I pass out.

At last, he says, "I don't know."

I glance up, so disappointed I could cry. I mean, I'd like to know one way or another, you know?

"But whether you are or not," he says, "what matters is this: that you accept and respect yourself for who you are."

He lowers his brow, all serious, but then smiles a little bit. "And you don't go punching people out about it. Is that clear?"

I nod, shifting nervously in my seat, my mind reeling.

"Anything else you want to ask?" he says.

I think for a moment and glance at the clock. "How long do I have to stay?"

"I think you've had enough for today." He tilts his head toward the door. "Tell your parents I'll call them tonight. You can start staying after school tomorrow."

Before he can utter another word, I grab my backpack. "See you," I yell behind me, sprinting into the hall. I'm not sure why I'm running, or why I feel so excited. I guess it's because of our conversation.

I fling open the building's front door and slam to a halt.

A lone figure sits on the balustrade, waiting. He glances up at me, his face scrunched, his brow worried-like. "Hey," Jamal says.

My skin tingles all over. Does this mean he's not angry? Are we still friends? Trying to stay calm, I say, "Hey."

His face relaxes. "How much time did you get?"

"A week's detention." I shrug, like I don't care, which I don't at this moment. I'm too crazy with excitement, wondering: Does this mean he didn't mind kissing?

"Curt got suspended," I tell Jamal.

"You sure smacked him good." Jamal grins, his tall lips spreading wide.

I smile a little in response and feel myself blush, even though I feel proud.

"You know," Jamal says, sounding serious again, "I didn't tell him anything, about . . ."

He means about us kissing at the movie.

"I know," I tell him.

Then he reaches out his arm for our combo handshake thing we do. And I know that in spite of all the last twenty-four hours' tears and fights and mega-chaos in my head, I'm bound to kiss him again, if he'll let me. Except this time, I hope neither of us pulls away.

I was thirteen when I first heard the word gay. *Immediately, I knew that's what I was. And I hated myself for it.*

Like so many gay, lesbian, bisexual, transgender, or questioning (GLBTQ) teens, I felt totally alone. I had no one to talk to, didn't know any openly gay people, and saw few representations of gays in the media.

The world and I have grown up a lot since then. TV shows like Will & Grace *and* Ellen *have brought positive portrayals of gays and lesbians into millions of homes, Gay-Straight Alliances have formed in thousands of schools, and many GLBTQ teens are "coming out" at ages as young as thirteen.*

Unfortunately, however, the predominant experience for most of the world's GLBTQ youth is still one of isolation, harassment, persecution, and self-loathing.

It's to those students and their allies that I dedicate this story. Hang in there. Know that you're not alone. The world is changing, and though you will be challenged, you can help make it better. Have courage. Be true to who you are. And never, ever, give up.

Peace,
Alex

Alex Sanchez

Alex Sanchez is the author of the novel *Rainbow Boys,* selected as a Best Book for Young Adults by the American Library Association, a Book for the Teen Age by the New York Public Library, and a finalist for the Lambda Literary Award. His most recent book is the sequel, *Rainbow High*.

Alex received his master's degree in guidance and counseling from Old Dominion University. For many years he worked as a counselor of youth and families both in the United States and overseas. Born in Mexico to parents of German and Cuban heritage, he currently resides in Virginia and on the Web at www.AlexSanchez.com.

Thirteen and a Half

Rachel Vail

All I knew about Ashley before I went over there yesterday was that until this year she went to private school and now she sits next to me in math. But she asked me over, and since I couldn't think of a good no, I said okay.

Ashley lives near school, so we walked. We didn't have a lot to talk about on the way, but she didn't seem to mind. She was telling me that when she grows up, she wants to be a veterinarian and a movie star and travel all over the world very glamorously and live life to the hilt. She asked if I like to live life to the hilt.

"I mostly just hang around," I admitted.

"But when you get older, and you can do anything," she whispered as we began climbing the steep steps up to her huge stone house. "What do you like to imagine?"

I was a little winded from the steps, so I just shrugged.

"Like, I am constantly imagining I can fly," said Ashley,

spreading her arms wide. "Do you ever imagine you're flying?"

I stopped for breath. "I sometimes imagine I'm in a bakery."

"Today is my half birthday," she said, pulling a key out of her shirt. It had been hanging from a shoelace around her neck. She bent close to the lock to use it. "Are you thirteen and a half yet?"

I shook my head. My birthday was just last month.

"It feels . . . you just feel . . . older, at thirteen and a half," she said. "Things shift, subtly. You'll see."

I followed her in. I think her house might actually be a mansion. The ceiling is very, very far from the floor in the room where you walk in. In my house we have a front hall. Ashley's you'd have to call a lobby. On the left there was a huge square room that I think was a library. Anyway, there were tons of books in there, on dark shelves all the way up to the ceiling. At the far end of the library, two huge doors opened into some other room. I don't know what room it was or if that one would open to another huge room. I decided to stay close to Ashley to avoid getting lost.

Ashley unzipped her jacket and dropped it on the floor, with her backpack still hooked through the sleeves. I took off my jacket and backpack, too, put them next to Ashley's, then followed Ashley past a dining room that had paintings of annoyed-looking people hanging on the greenish walls, down a long hallway, into the kitchen.

"What do you want for a snack?" asked Ashley.

I didn't know.

Ashley climbed up onto one of the counters and opened a cabinet. "Let's have Mallomars," she said. "I think you can tell a lot about a person by the way she eats Mallomars, don't you?"

She brought down the box and held it open for me to choose one. I picked one in the center of the back row, wondering what that revealed about me. She took one from the far right front and said, "Come on and meet my bird, Sweet Pea. Did I tell you I've had him since I turned three?"

My Mallomar was melting a little on my fingers as I hurried to keep up with Ashley, around corners and then up, up, up a steep flight of stairs with dark red carpeting worn out in the center of each step. My house is just regular.

"Sweet Pea is a budgie," Ashley was explaining. "People think that's the same as a parakeet, but it's not. Budgies are slightly larger and much more exotic. Do you like exotic animals?"

"Um," I said.

"I got Sweet Pea when I was three years old, and though, tragically, he never learned to talk people-language, he is still able to communicate, at least to me. I can tell his chirps apart. You'll see. This is my brother's room—don't go there," she warned, indicating a closed door. "This is the bathroom—do you have to go?"

"No."

"Okay. Tell me when you do."

I took a bite of my Mallomar, maybe revealing that I was a hungry type of person.

Ashley gripped a doorknob on a tall white door. "And this—this is my room."

She swung the door open. Everything inside was pink. Pink carpeting, pink walls, pink bed piled high with pink pillows. "Sweet Pea?" she called, heading across the thick rug toward an empty birdcage. "Sweet Pea? Ahhh!"

I got there as she began screaming, and I saw a dead bird, lying on its side at the bottom of the cage.

She was still screaming when a woman raced into the room, across the acres of pink rug, and grabbed Ashley, demanding, "What happened?"

Ashley stopped screaming, said, "Sweet Pea . . . died!" and started to sob. The woman, who, now that I got a better look, was an older version of Ashley—big brown eyes, freckled nose, black hair pulled back in a ponytail—anyway, the woman gathered Ashley into her arms and sat her down on the rug, hugging her.

I was still standing there, holding my half-eaten Mallomar, feeling a little weird. I don't think the woman, who I had to figure was Ashley's mom, even noticed I was there.

Ashley's crying turned from shrieks to gasps to, finally, just little burbles that sounded like she was saying, *Haboo.*

Her mom was stroking her hair, whispering, "Okay," and occasionally checking her watch.

I ate the rest of my Mallomar and tried not to look at

the dead bird or at Ashley and her mom, who seemed to be having some private time, just with me happening to be standing three feet away. I would've gone to the bathroom, but Ashley had said to tell her before I went there, so I thought maybe their family had a rule of some sort about that. They seemed like they might.

Ashley sniffled, then said, "I've had him since I was three." She whimpered a little, then dried her face on the bottom of her T-shirt. "It feels . . . it just feels like, like the death of my childhood."

"Oh, sweetheart," said the mom.

Ashley started sobbing again.

"Maybe I should call my mom," I whispered.

"Don't leave!" screamed Ashley.

So I didn't.

"I feel like," she started again. "I feel like maybe Sweet Pea felt like . . . like I had grown up, now that I turned thirteen and a half, and, like, after all this time, this lifetime together . . ." She was too breathy to continue.

"Ashley," said the mother. "There's something I have to tell you."

Ashley sat up straight, slid off her mother's lap, and sat cross-legged on the carpeting facing her mom. She swallowed hard and then nodded. "Okay."

"Sweet Pea," started the mom. "Sweet Pea wasn't actually, well, what you think he is. Or was."

"What do you mean?" asked Ashley.

"You didn't get this bird on your third birthday."

"Yes, I did," Ashley protested. "I remember. I went to the pet store with Grammy and Papa and picked him out."

"Well," said the mom, tilting her head sideways, "you picked out a bird. He looked something like Sweet Pea, and his name was Sweet Pea, too . . ."

"You mean . . ."

The mom scrunched her face apologetically. "You were so excited, but then the darn bird died a few weeks after we got him, and, well, I didn't want to start explaining death to a three-year-old, so I just went back to the pet store and got a new one."

"I can't believe you."

"Well," said the mom, "I didn't want you to be sad. And when that second one died, you were five and just starting kindergarten, so that seemed like a bad time to deal with death, too. So I just bought a new parakeet."

"Budgie."

"Isn't that the same as a parakeet?"

Ashley stared at her mother. "Budgies are more . . . Sweet Pea was a budgie."

"Not recently."

"There was more than one replacement?"

The mom smiled awkwardly. "Sweet Pea was sort of a series of birds."

"No!"

"Honey," said the mom, leaning toward Ashley, "some of them were green, some were blue. . . ."

"You said he was molting!" shrieked Ashley. "Get out!

Get out of my room! I want to be alone with Sweet Pea, or whoever this is! Get out!"

I wasn't sure if I was supposed to stay or go, but I followed the mom out just in case. Ashley didn't yell at me to stay, so I figured I'd made the right choice.

The mom closed the door behind us and said, "Do you want a snack? I am studying for the Bar."

I had no idea what that meant. I just shook my head.

"You can wait in the kitchen," she said, moving fast toward the stairs. I could see where Ashley gets her speed. "I'm sure Ashley will be down soon."

When we got down to the kitchen, the mom took out two glasses and a pitcher of water. She poured us each some, gulped hers down, then looked at me for the first time, really. "It's nice for Ashley that you are here. She was bound to discover death eventually, and it's nice she has a friend to lean on."

"I'm not really . . . we're not that close," I explained. "I just sit next to her in math."

"Well," said the mom, pouring herself more water, "I wish I could chat, but as I said, I really have to study. Call me if you and Ashley need anything."

And then she left. I sat alone in the kitchen listening to the clock tick, wondering if I should call my mom and ask her to pick me up early on account of the death of the bird and also since it was getting a little creepy there in Ashley's humongous kitchen all alone.

Just as I was starting to wander around to look for a phone, though, Ashley appeared in the doorway. She had a jewelry box in her hands. It was the kind where, when you open it, tinkly music plays and a ballerina spins on her toe. I had one of those when I was little.

"Want to do a funeral?" Ashley asked.

"Is he in there?" I asked.

Ashley nodded.

I followed her through the kitchen out into the backyard.

Across a big green lawn, up a hill toward some evergreen trees, we came to a shed. "Hold this," said Ashley, and handed me the jewelry box/coffin. I waited outside the shed while she went in. I tried to be very still so I wouldn't drop it. She came out wearing big denim gloves and holding a small spade.

"I don't have any experience with death," I told her.

"I didn't think I did, either," said Ashley. "I guess you never know."

I followed her to the evergreen trees. She knelt down beside one and started digging. I just stood there holding the jewelry box/coffin. When she was done, she said, "You can put him in."

"Do you—maybe you should," I suggested. "You're the one, you know . . ."

"That's okay," she said.

So I put the box into the hole.

"Kneel down with me," she whispered. "Please? I'll be quick."

"Okay." I knelt in the soft dirt. Usually at a friend's house we play Ping-Pong or something.

"I'm going to say some stuff, okay?"

I nodded.

Ashley took a deep breath. "Good-bye, Sweet Pea. I'm sorry I didn't realize you were actually a series of birds. I'm sorry if I wasn't a good enough bird owner and that you never learned to talk and you never flew anyplace interesting. I guess you probably had a pretty boring life. I'm sorry." She sniffled.

I was thinking she might start really crying again, and if she did, where would I find her mother? But she cleared her throat and turned to me. "Do you want to say anything?"

"Uh-uh."

"You can. Just say whatever comes to mind."

"I'm not that good at saying things," I whispered.

"That's okay," whispered Ashley. "He can't really hear you anyway."

I turned and looked at her. She was sort of smiling at me. I sort of smiled back. Ashley closed her eyes and lowered her head again.

I closed my eyes and said, "Okay. Sweet Pea? Um, I never knew you, you know, alive, but, and I don't really know Ashley that well either—I can't figure out if she is severely weird or, like, the opposite—but, um, I think she really, kind of, loved you."

"I did," mumbled Ashley. "I did."

"So," I continued, making it up as I went along, "I was thinking maybe it would be nice if you could, like, maybe show up in her dream some night and fly with her.

Because Ashley likes to imagine she's flying. Anyway, um, that's all."

Ashley stayed still with her eyes closed, so I didn't get up either. Sometime after my feet fell asleep, Ashley shoveled the dirt onto the top of the box and patted it down hard. Without saying anything, she got up and went back to the shed. I waited outside it again, stamping my pin-cushiony feet, until she came back out without the gloves and spade.

"Thanks," she said as we headed back toward her house. "That was really beautiful, what you said."

I shrugged.

She held the back door open for me. "Is this the worst play date of your life?"

"It's up there," I admitted.

We waited out front for my mom to pick me up. I sat between my stuff and Ashley. We both tilted our faces up toward the sun. When my mother's car pulled up and she beeped, I turned to Ashley. "Happy half birthday," I said.

"Thanks," she answered. "Thanks for, you know, being here today."

I grabbed my stuff and ran down the steps to my mom. I slipped into the car, buckled my seat belt, and leaned over to get my kiss.

"Did you have a good time?" Mom asked.

I shrugged. I looked out the window. Up the hill, on the front lawn, Ashley was running around in big, loose circles, her arms spread straight out.

When I was thirteen, sometimes I was fine, my old comfortable self: interested in everything, passionate about world events, eager to laugh or read or learn something new. But then, with increasing frequency, there were the other days. I was angry, misunderstood, melancholy. I was a little slow with the whole development *thing, so I had watched my friends, one by one, become awkward and moody, and I vowed,* Not me. *Until, suddenly, I was shocking myself with how awkward and moody—and fragile—I felt myself.*

I felt like I was on a boat: off balance and kind of lurchy/nauseated, though excited. And although I was eager to get where I was going (adulthood, or even teenager-hood, with all its power and passion), it was also difficult to watch my familiar childhood world grow more distant and less my own as I pulled away from its safe shore.

Plus I started to get pimples, which really cheered me up.

Rachel Vail

Rachel Vail is the author of The Friendship Ring series, as well as *Wonder, Do-Over, Daring to Be Abigail,* and *Ever After.* She has also written two picture books, *Over the Moon* and *Sometimes I'm Bombaloo,* and a series of chapter books called Mama Rex and T. She lives in New York City with her husband and two sons and a bird named Taylor. All her closest friends are at least a little weird.

Jeremy Goldblatt Is *So* Not Moses

James Howe

I Told You So

I told you Jeremy Goldblatt's bar mitzvah would be a joke. I knew we shouldn't go. I don't know why nobody listens to me. Didn't I tell them, "Mom, Dad, Jeremy Goldblatt is going to make a total fool of himself, okay? And I am going to make a total fool of myself just by being there." And now they have to admit I was right.

My mother said, "Chelsea, enough!" But then she said she was going to speak to the rabbi about the whole unfortunate incident.

The way I look at it? At least I got a new dress out of the deal.

Some People Grow Weird

Everybody's got an opinion about why Jeremy did it. Personally, I think he was trying to make some kind of weird statement. Adam B. says to me, "No way, Ben. You're giving him too much credit. Jeremy and Candy Andy? They're just a couple of nutcases who deserve each other." Adam L. says that Jeremy was being a leader, like Moses. Yeah, right. There's a lot I don't know, but one thing I know for sure: Jeremy Goldblatt is *so* not Moses.

Jeremy and the two Adams and me, we go back a long ways. We were all friends once, but then Jeremy got weird somewhere around fifth grade, and the two Adams and me, we kind of had to cut him from the lunch table. Don't get all, like, "How could you do that?" because it's not like we're bad guys or anything. It's just that Jeremy got to be an embarrassment. Some people grow up and some people grow weird, okay? Jeremy grew weird.

Ben Isn't Always Right

When Ben and Adam B. and Jeremy and me were kids, we would hang out together and have so much fun. Jeremy always came up with the greatest games, ones he thought up by himself that were really complicated and interesting, a fact that now amazes me to think about. I really felt bad when Ben said we had to cut him from the lunch table and stop hanging around with him and all. I don't know how it happened, but Ben just got to be in charge at some point, and he told Jeremy he didn't like how he was always saying we had to do this and we had to do that. I guess because *Ben* wanted to be the one saying we had to do this and we had to do that.

I still like Jeremy, it's just hard to be his friend. Some of that's because of Jeremy himself. I mean, it's true what Ben said—he did get weird. Or maybe he just *seemed* weirder as we got older. I don't know if he's really weird so much as he's just kind of slow. Anyway, he gets teased a lot, and that's the other reason it's hard to be his friend.

This past year, I've been going to a whole bunch of bar and bat mitzvahs. I'm not Jewish, but I have a lot of friends who are. I'll tell you one thing: I'm glad I didn't have to have a bar mitzvah when I turned thirteen, because it's a lot of work. You have to read from the Bible, except when it's Jewish, it's called the Torah. And it isn't even the whole Bible and it isn't even a book, it's a big parchment scroll on wooden rollers. And the words are all in Hebrew. The Torah is like this major sacred object. It's a big deal just to touch it. Anyway, you have to read what's called a "portion" from it—*in Hebrew*—and then you have to give a speech. And that's just *some* of what you have to do. Adam B. and Ben, they say it's worth it because you get to have a cool party and all these presents, but Jeremy said he didn't care about that so much as doing a good job. Ben and Adam B. laughed at him and said, "Okay, Germy, whatever you say."

I guess Jeremy was worried about doing a good job because of his brother Neil's bar mitzvah being legendary and all. And, like I said, he's kind of slow. It's sometimes embarrassing when he gets up to read or talk in school. Kids laugh. Ben laughs the loudest. He laughed at Jeremy at his bar mitzvah, too.

Sometimes I have to wonder why I'm still Ben's friend.

I'm Only the Mother

I've been trying to get some sense out of Jeremy since it happened, but he just sits in front of his computer grunting until I threaten to pull the plug right out of the wall. Then he turns around and says to me, "I don't understand you, Mom. You should be proud of me."

Proud? I should be proud of him?

My husband says, "Denise, let it go."

I say, "Michael, we just spent thirty thousand dollars on a natural disaster, and we can't even apply for government relief. I'm supposed to let that go?"

Michael nods at me and does his little *mm-hmm* thing, which he knows drives me up the wall. Sometimes I think he and Jeremy should move into a high-tech cave together so they can grunt and play with their supersonic toys to their hearts' content.

Why do I even bother? I mean, it's Michael's money. Yes, I have a part-time career, but let's be honest, it's mostly Michael's money that pays for things. If he wants to throw away thirty thousand dollars, who am I to care?

I'm only the mother.

Watch me. I'm going to go into the kitchen right now, put on an apron, and bake a kugel.

The Wise of Heart

I've been a rabbi for over twenty years—twenty-two to be exact—and I've got to tell you, I never in my life enjoyed a bar mitzvah as much as Jeremy Goldblatt's. I'll admit I wasn't sure he would be able to rise to the occasion. Let's face it, the boy has nowhere near the brains of his big brother. Neil's bar mitzvah was three years ago, and people are still talking about it. He led the service as if *he* were the rabbi. At the end of it, I didn't know whether to cheer or hand him the keys to my office. Meanwhile, Jeremy sat there in the front row the whole time, hunched over like the little unformed lump of clay he was, and I could tell what he was thinking: In three years, it'll be *me* up there.

Poor kid, having to follow an act like Neil's.

The thing is, Jeremy may not have his brother's smarts or charisma or leadership qualities, but he's got something Neil can't touch. Jeremy, he's one of the *chochmei halev*, the "wise of heart." You know what he said to me at our first meeting? He said, "Rabbi, how do I make my bar mitzvah *mean* something?"

Do you hear what I'm telling you? A rabbi lives for words like that.

The month before Jeremy's bar mitzvah, I had Chelsea Balter-Minter's bat mitzvah. When it was time for her Torah commentary, she compared the Israelites' wandering in the desert to the time she and her mother got lost in the parking lot at the Mall of America. I kid you not.

Born to Shop

Poor Rabbi Sandler. He told me I shouldn't talk about my family's excursion to the Mall of America in my Torah commentary, and I told him, "Rabbi, I was born to shop." He laughed. Like he thought I was joking or something.

He doesn't understand that in my personal view shopping is the spiritual experience of our times. He also doesn't understand that I speak the language of my peers. I reach them when I talk—unlike Jeremy Goldblatt, who may as well be an undiscovered planet, he is so far out in space.

The only reason I was invited to Jeremy's bar mitzvah in the first place is because his parents and mine were friends when we moved here from the city, so Jeremy and I were friends, too. (If you tell anybody that, I swear you will be in *so* much trouble.) I mean, fine, when Jeremy was little, he was cute and all, and we did things like share Popsicles and play in the sandbox and ride our bikes with training wheels around the block. But that is *no* reason to invite someone to a bar mitzvah.

That was years ago. History. Jeremy went his way, and I went mine.

The Problem

I am not a bigot, but I went to talk to Rabbi Sandler before Chelsea's bat mitzvah, and now, after the travesty that took place at Jeremy's bar mitzvah, I am clearly going to have to speak to him again. The man just does not seem to get it.

Anyway, when I met with him, I got right to the point. I said, "David, what are you going to do about the problem?"

He said, "Shelley, I don't know what problem you're referring to."

"Oh, please, Dave," I said. "You know very well I'm talking about the *person* who sits in the back row every *Shabbas* and *hums*. And *smells*. As far as I know, he is not a member of our congregation."

"No, he's not," the rabbi said matter-of-factly. "And, by the way, he has a name. It's Andy."

I leaned forward and whispered, "Is he Jewish?"

"I have no idea. He's a human being, that's all I need to know. And he's welcome here."

"Excuse me for saying, Rabbi, but this is a synagogue, not a shelter."

"What is a synagogue *but* a shelter?" Rabbi Sandler asked.

Well, I had nothing to say to that. I just hate it when he gets all *rabbinical*. I changed my strategy.

"How's Claire?" I asked. "And the kids?"

"They're fine," he said. "Shelley, I understand your concern. You don't want Andy making a scene and embarrassing you and your family at Chelsea's bat mitzvah. I appreciate that. It's a very special day, and you want it to be perfect."

"Perfect," I repeated. "Exactly."

"You know, Chelsea's Torah portion reminds us that we were strangers in the land of Egypt."

"I am well aware of Chelsea's Torah portion, Dave. I've been working on it with her for months. However, I don't see what it has to do with—"

"It has everything to do with Andy," he went on. I didn't think it was very rabbinical of him to interrupt me and assume he knew what I was going to say. Even if he *did* know. "Andy is a stranger in our midst. Remembering what it was like to be strangers ourselves, we cannot turn him away. On the contrary—"

"Please," I said, putting up my hand.

He shrugged. "Let me do this. I will speak to Andy about behaving properly at Chelsea's bat mitzvah. He's a sick man, Shelley. He can't always control his fidgeting or his humming. But he isn't going to hurt anyone, I can assure you of that. For some reason, he feels at home here, and he truly wants to behave well. I try to encourage that. I'll remind him again. And I'll intervene if there's a problem. Is that agreeable?"

"It isn't exactly what I was hoping for, but I guess it will have to do."

"Thanks, Shelley. And please say hello to Jeff for me. I'd love to see him at services more often."

I swear, Rabbi Sandler is like his own TV show. There are *always* commercial interruptions.

Candy Andy and Me

Sometimes Candy Andy sits out on the steps in front of the synagogue. He's usually eating a candy bar, which is how come most of the kids call him Candy Andy. He's not very old, even though a lot of them say he is.

I've been going to Hebrew school here for a whole bunch of years, just like my brother, Neil, did before me. I go to school with most of these kids. Regular school, I mean. Except for Stuart Mandelbaum, who has B.O. and a fear of anything with more than two legs, I don't have any friends here. I don't have many what you'd call "friends" anywhere, ever since Ben and the two Adams dumped me in the fifth grade. I try to keep in with them, but they make it pretty clear they don't want me around.

Ben and Adam B., they call me Germy and say things like, "Okay, Germy, now be a good boy and go away," whenever I say something to them on the bus or something. Adam L. is nicer to me and actually comes over to my house sometimes. But only when Ben and Adam B. aren't around.

I don't really understand what happened. To Ben and the two Adams and me, I mean.

Anyway, I was going to tell you about Candy Andy and me.

The first time I talked to Candy Andy was one afternoon when my mom was late picking me up and Chelsea Balter-Minter and I were the only ones left waiting. Ben and Adam B. had already been picked up by Adam B.'s dad, and of course they didn't say good-bye or anything. It wasn't like I was expecting Chelsea to talk to me, either, even though we were the only ones left and she and I had been friends once, too.

We just sat there on the steps, staring off in the same direction, looking at the same things probably, but not talking. I knew her bat mitzvah was coming up soon, and I wanted to ask if she was nervous about it, because I was nervous about mine. But I didn't want her saying anything that would make me feel bad about myself, so I just kept quiet.

At one point, I dug into my backpack and found a 3 Musketeers bar. I think a 3 Musketeers bar should be split three ways. It just should. So I worked up the nerve and asked Chelsea if she wanted a third. She surprised me by saying yes. I looked around to see who I could give the other third to, and that's when I noticed Candy Andy sitting there.

"You're not going to give it to *him*, are you?" Chelsea asked, wrinkling her nose as if I'd just spit on her shoe or something.

"Why not?"

She didn't answer, just turned away so she wouldn't have to watch.

"Hi," I said, going over to Candy Andy. "Do you want a third of this 3 Musketeers bar?" I broke off a piece and held it out to him.

He looked me over good, as if he was making sure I wasn't trying to trick him. That gave me a chance to look him over, too. That's when I noticed he wasn't much older than my parents. He had a nice face, one that looked kind of beaten up, but it wasn't hard or mean. I thought at first he had angry eyes, but then I realized they were more like a scared animal's.

I sat down next to him. He smelled, but so does Stuart Mandelbaum, and I've never held that against *him*.

We started eating our 3 Musketeers thirds together,

staring off into space, looking at the same things in the distance, just the way Chelsea and I had been doing. But it felt better doing it with Candy Andy than with Chelsea. That made me feel sad at first, like, Oh my God, I have more in common with a crazy, smelly, homeless guy than I do with a so-called normal person, but then I decided to ride the good feeling and let go of the sad one. I mean, what's "normal," anyway?

"Those are nice trees over there," I said. He didn't answer, but I could tell he was listening, so I went on. I said whatever I felt like since I didn't think he'd say anything back. And I wasn't really sure how much he understood. "Do you think it matters to be Jewish? Do you think God cares if you're Jewish or Catholic or an atheist or whatever? My mom and dad are so psyched about this bar mitzvah, I feel like I have to prove to them that I'm as good as Neil. But I don't think God cares if I'm good at anything except maybe being good. I mean, what kind of God would care if you give a good speech or get a whole bunch of presents or invite lots of kids just to prove you're popular? And if God doesn't care, then what's the point? Who am I supposed to be pleasing, anyway? I think the point of having a bar mitzvah is to go through something that *means* something so you'll know the difference between being a child and being an adult. 'Cause that's what it's supposed to be about, you know, growing up. But I'm not sure I get it. If I knew I could do something that would *mean* something, then maybe I'd understand what happened with

Ben and the two Adams and why kids make fun of me and stuff like that. I know that doesn't make much sense, but—"

"That was good," Candy Andy said.

I think he was talking about the 3 Musketeers.

When I heard my mom's car horn, I stood up and brushed off my pants, which is something I always do, and said, "Well, I'll see ya."

"That will be fine with me," Candy Andy said.

Different

Okay, this is going to sound really shallow, but I would *so* hate to be different. I mean, I don't know how people who are different can stand it. I first had this thought when I was sitting in front of temple that time Jeremy offered me a piece of his candy bar. Ordinarily, I do not eat chocolate or any kind of sugared food, but, well, nobody was around, so what the hell.

Anyway, he was so sweet, the way he asked, that I could almost see being his friend again. I mean, not really, of course, but I remembered what he was like when we were little, and, I don't know, I just felt sort of sad because of how things change. So there I was, kind of opening up my soul to him and all—not that he knew—when he goes over and sits down next to that creepy guy who's always hanging around the synagogue.

And I couldn't help staring at them, you know? It's kind of like a car wreck. It's really gruesome and all, but you can't stop looking. So I'm staring, and my sad feeling got worse and worse, 'cause I thought how awful it must be to be different and have nobody like you, and how you can't do anything about it because it's just the way you are. And then I wondered if Jeremy would end up like that guy, Candy Andy, you know, crazy and out in the streets and all.

And I felt just awful. And I began to pray—honest to God, *pray*—that my mother would get there soon to pick me up and where the hell was she anyway?

A Tube of Toothpaste

From my office window, I watched Jeremy sit and talk with Andy each week after Hebrew school. On days when there was no Hebrew school, Jeremy still came by from time to time, just to sit with Andy and talk to him. I never knew what the two of them talked about, or if Andy ever spoke at all, but I did notice that at some point Jeremy would take out a candy bar and share it with Andy. On his fifth or sixth visit, he brought Andy a toothbrush and a tube of toothpaste.

Meanwhile, Jeremy was struggling with his Hebrew. I kept shortening his Torah portion so he'd have less to memorize. I knew how much he wanted to do well, but I also knew that just getting through the service without messing up might be as much as he could manage.

As I worked with Jeremy, I grew to like him more and more. I'd rarely known such a sweet kid. For the life of me, I couldn't understand why he was an outcast among his peers. But then I remembered what it was like when

I was his age, how cruel my friends could be. How cruel I must have been, too.

Perhaps in the land of the cruel, the wise heart cannot be tolerated.

Faith

I don't know why I started spending so much time with Candy Andy. It wasn't like he had much to say. But he *was* a good listener. Still, hanging out with him sure didn't help my social status any. Even Stuart Mandelbaum told me I was a loser. *Stuart Mandelbaum.*

One day, after Andy and I had finished off a Baby Ruth, I got to talking about Moses and how he'd had a pretty hard life, too. "If his mother hadn't hidden him in a basket in the river," I told Andy, who was staring off into space as usual, "he wouldn't have made it even to *kindergarten.* If they had kindergarten back then. I mean, the Pharaoh wanted him *dead.* And here's something I'll bet you didn't know: Moses was 'slow of speech.' Rabbi Sandler told me. You know what Moses said to God? 'Pick somebody else to lead the people. I'm slow of speech.' That's funny, right? But God isn't somebody who takes no for an answer. He told Moses he had to lead the people, whether he wanted to or not. He said, 'I'm the one who made you the way you are, so I'll stick by you and help you figure out what to say.' So Moses did what God told him. That's called faith. Do you have faith, Andy?"

"Baby Ruth, God is truth," Andy said.

I laughed. I never knew Andy could be funny before that.

Such Good Boys

Nana always says, "You and Jeremy, you're such good boys." Grandmothers are supposed to say things like that, I guess, but I think Nana actually believes it. Maybe all grandmothers do.

The year leading up to Jeremy's bar mitzvah, our mother was like this out-of-control windup toy that kept hitting the wall and falling apart. Nana was always the one who put her back together.

"All that matters is Jeremy," she would say. "Stop with the lists already, Denise. Who cares about the invitations and the flowers and the caterer? They'll be fine. And so will Jeremy."

"Oh, really?" Mom would say. "How is he going to be fine? He can't remember his Hebrew. You can't hear him when he speaks. He walks around with his mouth hanging open, for God's sake."

"If he walks around with his mouth hanging open for God's sake, then God must want it that way," Nana would answer.

That Nana, she is one funny lady.

And a good one, too.

To the rest of my family, I'm the star. When I take home an A or win a game, Mom and Dad get all pumped up about it. Even Jeremy, who's got every reason to hate me, says, "Cool."

But Nana, she always says something like, "Good for you, Neil. And did Jeremy show you what his teacher wrote on his story last week? 'Fine work!' What did I do to deserve two such grandsons?"

At Jeremy's bar mitzvah, Nana was the only one in the family who didn't go nuts. She was the one who said to him after, "That was a good thing you did, Jeremy. Don't let anybody tell you otherwise. You and your brother, you're such good boys."

Who Needs to Breathe?

All right. First of all, I put on three pounds the week before. Second, had I bothered to try on my new dress in over a month? Of course not. I put it on that morning and said, "Michael, I can't breathe." He said, "Denise, you'll be so happy you won't need to breathe." So . . . third, it fit like a straitjacket, which . . . fourth, is what I was thinking would have been a good thing to have handy because . . . fifth, that crazy man was in the back row humming and smelling and swaying in his seat.

Shelley Balter had warned me, but had I listened? No. I said, "Shelley, Candy Andy is the least of my worries."

Which at first I thought was true since all I could think about was Jeremy.

I kept motioning to him to speak up, and I mouthed the words when he stumbled over his Hebrew. But once I realized he was going to get through this without my help, I started paying attention to what else was going on. That's when I heard the humming and rustling coming from the back of the sanctuary. I turned to Michael and said, "Michael, do something about you-know-what."

He said, "What am I supposed to do?" Which is better than *mm-hmm*, but not much.

"Get the rabbi's attention," I hissed.

"He's running a service here," Michael replied, a little too loudly.

"Well then, go over to the man yourself and ask him to leave."

"I can't do that, Denise. Besides which, you know Jeremy *wanted* him here."

"What Jeremy wants—"

"It's *his* bar mitzvah," Michael said in this reprimanding tone. I hate it when my husband sounds just like my mother.

But I had the last laugh, didn't I?

Not that I was laughing.

Jeremy's Guest

It was during the Torah reading that I noticed how agitated Andy was getting. I began preparing myself to have a word with him.

I'm not going to lie to you. I have never been confident that I've handled the "Andy problem" as well as I might. He can be disturbing, it's true, but he's never so disturbing that I have to ask him to leave. I came to the conclusion some time ago that it was the *idea* of Andy that upset people more than the reality. Why is it so hard to accept someone who is so different? More times than I can remember I've said the words, "You shall not oppress a stranger, for you know the feelings of the stranger."

And more than once, I've gotten the response, "But you're allowing this man to oppress *us*."

I've never been sure what to say to that.

When Denise Goldblatt called me the week before Jeremy's bar mitzvah, however, I knew exactly what to say. "Denise, I was standing right next to Jeremy when he handed Andy one of your beautifully engraved invitations and asked him, 'Andy, will you please come to my bar mitzvah?'"

She wasn't happy about it, but what could she say? Andy was going to be there as Jeremy's guest.

Now, guest or not, I could see I was going to have to do something, as more members of the congregation were looking over their shoulders at the man in the last row who was humming loudly, rocking back and forth, and picking at his shirt.

Just as I was going to make my move, Jeremy tugged at my sleeve and asked, "Rabbi, before we put the Torah away, could I carry it around the sanctuary?"

We often carry the Torah around the sanctuary during Saturday-morning services, but we hadn't planned on doing it that particular morning. Lack of planning didn't seem a good enough reason to say no, however. And besides, walking around the sanctuary would give me an ideal opportunity to stop and have a word with Andy. I nodded and handed the Torah to Jeremy, who nearly fell over from the unexpected weight of it. The congregation chuckled, while I began thinking of what I would say when we reached the back row.

Jeremy led our small procession around the room as many of the congregants touched their prayer books to the scroll and brought them back to their lips. We were surrounded by the lovely sound of prayers and blessings for Jeremy and the Torah, made only slightly less lovely by Andy's tuneless buzz-saw humming cutting through it all. I could see Denise desperately trying to make eye contact with me, and I finally smiled at her, hoping she would know I was on my way to quiet Andy down.

As we rounded the back of the sanctuary, the congregation fell silent. Everyone's eyes shifted from Jeremy and the Torah to Andy, whose own eyes were clamped shut. He was standing now, swaying while he hummed. There was no way I could talk to him without making a scene. I wasn't sure what to do, when Jeremy suddenly took the decision from me.

Stopping abruptly in front of Andy, he held out the Torah. "Here," he said. "Take the Torah, Andy. Walk with us."

Several people gasped as my mind began to reel at the thought of the phone calls I'd be getting.

Andy's eyes popped open. He stopped humming and looked wildly into Jeremy's face.

"Here," Jeremy repeated, thrusting the Torah at him. "Come on. I want you to."

Andy grabbed the Torah and swung it high over his

head. I didn't know if he was going to beat somebody with it or send it flying.

He didn't do either. He shouted at the top of his lungs, "Baby Ruth, God is truth!" And then he began to dance.

Looney Tunes

Maybe it would have been okay if he'd shouted it just once, but Andy kept repeating it over and over—"Baby Ruth, God is truth!"—as he swung the Torah in wide circles over his head and did this funky dance. The people nearby were ducking and screaming, and other people were laughing. Rabbi Sandler kept saying, "Andy, Andy, please give me the Torah." But there was no way Andy was giving it back.

I know I should have been thinking, Handing the Torah to Candy Andy was the stupidest thing I ever did in my whole life!

But I wasn't. I was thinking, Way to go, Andy!

Because you should have seen him. He was so happy. Like this little kid at a party. The next thing you know, he stopped shouting and started singing. His voice is weird and raspy, but this time there was something really beautiful about it. I don't know why, but I got this picture in my head of all these birds flying up out of his throat and soaring into the sky. Like they'd just been set free or something. The sound of it made me so happy, I started singing, too.

Ben called out, "Looney tunes!" But I didn't care.

When Andy heard me singing, he brought the Torah down and clutched it to his heart like it was his baby or something, and then he grabbed me with his other hand and shouted, "Come on, Jeremy, come on! Dance!"

So I did.

Andy and me, we danced all around the sanctuary, singing our looney tunes—which didn't have any words—and moving however our feet told us to move. And you know what happened? People started clapping, and pretty soon the rabbi was shouting, "Everybody, join in!"

And then we were one big circle, holding hands and dancing and singing looney tunes that had no words.

Everybody was in the circle.

Even Chelsea.

Even Ben and the two Adams.

Even my mother, though she didn't look happy about it.

Even Nana, who winked at me.

Even Andy.

Even me.

The Truth

All I can say is, thank God Jeremy Goldblatt's bar mitzvah is over and people will have other things to talk about and won't keep asking me, "Did you hear?" And I won't have to keep saying, "Hear? I was *there*!" And they won't keep looking at me like, *Ooh, you were there?* Like, *Ooh, who are you, anyway, Chelsea Balter-Minter?*

If you want to know the truth (and if you tell anybody this, I swear I will *so* never speak to you again), sometimes

I'm not so sure who I am anymore. Like, for instance, when we started dancing around the synagogue and singing that stupid la-la-la song, I thought I was going to *die*, it was so embarrassing. But then there was this other part of me that thought . . . well, I'm going to be brutally honest now: This is so *fun*!

I can't believe I told you that.

You see what I mean? I don't know what to think anymore. I *hate* that. I used to know what to think about everything.

Okay, here's another example. I still think Jeremy is weird, and there's no way I could be his friend or anything. But there's something *different* about him since his bar mitzvah. *Good* different. He seems, I don't know, more grown up or something. Not so out in space. And it's not like I *like* him all of a sudden. But I guess maybe I respect him.

Yesterday, we were sitting out on the front steps of the synagogue, waiting to be picked up. Out of nowhere, Jeremy said, "Do you remember how we shared Popsicles when we were little?" I told him I did. I was hoping he wouldn't mention the time I licked his arm where his Popsicle had dripped. He didn't, and then I felt bad thinking maybe he didn't remember.

He took out a 3 Musketeers and offered me a third. I started to say yes, but then my mother drove up and I didn't want her yelling at me for eating chocolate. But as I got in the car I noticed him heading over to Candy Andy and I thought: A 3 Musketeers should be split three ways. It just should. So I called out, "Jeremy, I'll take a third."

You should have seen the smile on his face when he handed it to me.

Candy Andy waved at me as we drove away.

And then you know what happened? I waved back.

Me. Chelsea Balter-Minter. I waved good-bye to Candy Andy.

I told you I don't know what to think anymore.

And that's the truth.

One of my memories of being thirteen is of the hours spent hanging out on my next-door neighbor's front porch, engaged in heated debates about religion and the nature of faith. The son of a liberal Baptist minister, I was raised to ask challenging questions and grapple with my beliefs. My neighbor—and my best friend at the time—was twelve, Catholic, and something of an independent thinker. His two sisters—one older and one younger—were shocked by our conversations, yet could rarely tear themselves away. They always came to the same conclusion: We were doomed to eternal damnation. (Especially me.)

My spiritual questioning continued long after my neighbor moved away a year or two later. At the age of thirty-two, it led to my decision to convert to Judaism. Having attended many bar and bat mitzvahs in the years since, I've often thought about those lively debates I had with my neighbor. I've wondered if other twelve- and thirteen-year-olds sit around talking about such things. I've asked myself what it means to stand up at the age of thirteen and make a public statement about one's faith—or one's uncertainty. What does it matter? And what do faith and religion have to do with the rest of one's life—with school, for example, or friends or family?

I gave these questions to Jeremy Goldblatt, a boy who, like many of the characters in my books and stories, is an outsider. Jeremy has good reasons to ask questions. Being an outsider rarely makes sense. Jeremy's recognition of the unfairness dealt a fellow outsider leads him from questioning to action. In the process, he discovers that the connective tissue between the two is meaning.

Finding meaning, of course, is the reason for all the questions in the first place. It's the reason I wrote this story. It's the reason I write.

James Howe

James Howe is the author of more than sixty books for young readers. His first book, *Bunnicula*, remains one of his most popular and best-selling titles. In addition to *Bunnicula*'s sequels, he has written a series of short chapter books, Tales from the House of Bunnicula. His many books for younger readers include the Pinky and Rex series and the picture books *Horace and Morris but Mostly Dolores* and *There's a Monster Under My Bed*. He is the author of two novels for young adults: *The Watcher* and *The Misfits*. Set in the seventh grade, *The Misfits* tells the story of four best friends who set out to end name-calling in their school. He is the editor of one other short-story collection for young adults, *The Color of Absence: 12 Stories About Loss and Hope*.

Black Holes and Basketball Sneakers

Lori Aurelia Williams

Malik slung his backpack over his shoulder and sprinted across the empty schoolyard. He reached the back chain-link fence, climbed over it, and dropped down onto the cracked sidewalk. A moment later a chorus of angry male voices rang out behind him.

"Hey, Malik, where you think you going, punk? You better wait up!"

Malik swallowed hard and hurried toward the busy intersection, but even as he reached the red stoplight, he knew that he was just wasting his time. Jamar and his boys would never give up. They would follow him just a baby step from his apartment if they had to, follow him and make his life miserable.

It's what the boys had done since the day Malik started at Matthew Henderson Junior High. It was raining that day, raining enough cats and dogs for five pet stores. Malik had gotten to school hungry because his five sisters had eaten all the cornflakes and late because he had to drop his baby sister, Mara, off at her day care. By the time he made it to his class wing, his stomach was grumbling like he hadn't eaten since Jesus broke bread at the Last Supper, and he was drenched. That's what started the problem, not the annoying rumble in his belly, which he had no choice but to get used to from time to time—it was Mother Nature's tears. They got all up in his sneakers, and as soon as he stepped foot in the tile hallway, his shoes started to squish and squeak like his baby sister's plastic rubber duck did when she played with it in the bathtub. His social studies class heard him long before he reached the classroom, and when he finally pulled open the wooden door to go inside, thirty pairs of dark brown eyes fell on him—and his sneaks.

In that moment Malik wished he could sprout giant wings like Morph Man, the superhero on the only Saturday-morning cartoon that he still watched. If he could have changed the genetic code in his DNA like Morph Man, he would have soared right through the closed classroom window, shattering the glass and leaving nothing but shards to remember him by. That way, the other kids wouldn't have had time to see the faded blue canvas sneakers that his mom had purchased from the discount store almost two years ago. They wouldn't have noticed the huge holes on the sides that his toes sometimes poked through, or the way the tattered material virtually disintegrated near the bottoms, leaving his soles to flap open with each step. But Malik wasn't a superhero. He was just a thirteen-year-old kid whose mother didn't make jack serving steaming bowls of chili down at Enrique's Chili and Taco joint. So Malik had to take it. "Say, man, what you been walking through, holy water? 'Cause it's more holes in them raggedy shoes you got on than in a golf course," a rough-looking boy with his kinky hair braided real close to his skull had yelled. The other kids had all laughed. Malik had felt terrible, and the boy, who he later learned was called Jamar, made certain that he stayed feeling that way. The second the bell rang, Jamar and his crew had surrounded him in the hallway and shot the dozens on him until he wished he had never come to the new school, never even come out of his mother's womb.

"Hey, Malik! You better wait up or else, punk!"

Malik stopped. There was no point in even trying to make it across the street. He dropped his hands to his sides and waited.

Three boys came racing up. Malik clenched his fists but stood still. He was short for his age, and the boys were all taller and bigger than him. Over their blue jeans they wore navy muscle shirts, and on their feet they wore brand-new shiny white leather sneakers trimmed in red suede. Malik didn't even bother checking out the black name sewn into the sides of the shoes. He knew what the shoes were. JC Jumpers. The new sneaks that all the kids in school had—except him.

"Hey, Malik, where you going so fast? You don't want

to hang with us?" Jamar asked. He grabbed the front of Malik's shirt and pulled Malik to him. Jamar's breath was kicking hard from the Kool cigarettes he liked to smoke between classes. Malik struggled free and took a deep breath.

"Aw, man, you know that boy can't talk. He too soft to open his mouth," said Wayne, a pug-nosed boy with eyes so squinty Malik couldn't tell if they were open or closed. He sometimes wondered how Wayne made it through the day without bumping into everything.

"I know what you talking about, bro. He can't walk, either, with them raggedy sneaks he got on," said Hendrix, the third boy, who was wearing enough silver chains around his thick neck to open up his own jewelry stand.

Wayne kicked one of Malik's sneakers. Malik glanced down at his feet and back up at Wayne, but he still didn't say anything. Jamar was tough, but Wayne was a brother you really didn't want to mess with. His first week at their junior high school Malik saw Wayne slam a boy's head into his locker just because the boy teased him about a low test score.

Jamar narrowed his huge eyes and grabbed Malik by the shirt again. "Go on and say something, dog," he said. "Why you acting like you scared and stuff? What, you some kinda titty baby? You need some mama's milk?"

"Aw, man, his mama ain't got no milk to spare with all them hungry mugs she got to feed. Say, bro, tell your mama they got something new now called 'the pill.' Tell her to take her sorry behind on down to the clinic. They'll hook a sister right up," Wayne said.

Malik gritted his teeth. "Leave my mama alone," he said.

"I ain't leaving nobody alone. I hear ain't none of ya'll Negroes even got the same last name."

"That's 'cause she probably don't even know what last name to give any of 'em. I bet she done had mo' dudes under her hood than my grandma's old Plymouth," Hendrix said with an ugly laugh.

Malik completely lost it. "Don't be talking about my mama!" he yelled.

"What you gonna do, punk?" Jamar yelled.

"I—I—I don't want to fight you," Malik said, shaking violently. "Just lay off of my mama."

"Well, what you gonna do about it? Go on, swang if you gonna swang, punk," Wayne said, moving in. "What you waiting on? Go on and beat him down," he said to Jamar. "Give him a reason to run back home to his mama, since he likes her so much."

Wayne pushed Jamar against Malik's chest. Malik closed his eyes and waited for the other boy to start pounding him. It didn't happen. Malik opened his eyes to see his neighbor Carl, an enormous ninth grader with the bulging muscles of a middleweight boxer, standing over them.

"Hey, Malik. You all right, man?" Carl stepped in between Malik and the other boys and pushed Malik behind him. "Hey, man, why ya'll always got to push up on somebody who can't fight back?" Carl asked the three boys. "Why don't ya'll act a fool with somebody that can beat ya'll down for a change?"

"What you care, man? Why you always dipping in other folks' business?" Wayne yelled. "Why don't you get some business of your own?"

"Look, punk, anything I say is my business—is my business. You got that?" Carl grabbed Wayne by the throat and shoved him to the pavement. Wayne's eyes flamed, but he stayed put.

"Don't mess with me, Wayne," Carl said. "'Cause I'll take all you young punks out." Next he grabbed Jamar by the front of his muscle shirt.

"Let me go, man," Jamar begged. "Come on, Carl, man, be cool. Ain't nobody trying to fight you."

"I know ain't nobody trying to fight me," Carl said, twisting his shirt tightly. "But ya'll ain't trying to fight nobody else, either, are you?"

Jamar started shaking his head quickly. His huge brown eyes were saturated with fear. "Naw," he said. "Naw, Carl. Let me go. We about to step off. Just turn me loose, dog."

Carl did as he asked. Jamar and Hendrix bent down and helped Wayne to his feet. The three boys bailed.

"That's what I'm talking about!" Carl yelled at their fleeing backs. "You better get your gangster wanna-be behinds outta here before I mess all of ya'll up."

"Just wait till next time, Malik!" Malik thought he heard Jamar's voice trail. He dabbed at the corner of his wet eyes with his fingers, noticing for the first time the fear-tears that had formed there.

"You okay, man?" Carl asked. "Look, bro, don't waste no water over them thugs. Put yourself on a higher plane, dog. Don't let no sorry dudes bring you down. You just walk away with your pride, and don't give them another thought."

Malik nodded. "I will. I'll try. It's just that they keep sweatin' me over my shoes," he said, looking down at the expanding holes in the canvas.

"Yeah, man, I'm sorry about that. Dudes like that, they always got to have somebody to pick on," Carl said, glancing down at his own black leather JC Jumpers. "I know how it is, man. I used to be just like you, before I hooked up with the Bullets. My mama was on that stuff, so my grandma took me in. She cool and all, but she ain't never had enough money to buy a Happy Meal. Some fool was always getting on me about my hand-me-down threads. I was in a fight after school almost every day, but that got tired, dog. Even though I could handle myself, *it got tired.* So I hooked up with the Bullets. They been real cool to me. Sometimes they just like I would want my mama to be, and now I ain't got nothing at all to worry about. You see what I got on, don't you, little bro?"

Malik checked out Carl's sneaks and his fly navy blue FUBU T-shirt and baggy jeans. When he finally pulled his eyes away, he forced himself to smile weakly.

"Don't be jealous, little bro," Carl said. "You can have all of this, too. Just come over to Sandra's anytime you get ready. I'll get the guys to hook you up. We'll give Jamar and his crew something to get all green in the face about."

"Okay, thanks," Malik said timidly, feeling a bit guilty.

Carl nodded. "It ain't nothing but a thang, little bro. Well, I got to get to stepping. Later for you, dog." He slapped Malik on the shoulder and ran back toward the schoolyard.

On the way back to his place Malik thought a lot about Carl. He didn't know much about him, but he already knew that he was definitely a stand-up brother, always around when you needed him. Carl was the kind of guy who was always doing stuff for other folks around the hood, helping the old ladies tote their overflowing baskets of dirty laundry to the washroom, even mowing lawns for the single mothers who lived in the rent shacks across the street from their project.

But he didn't know about Carl's invitation to hang out with the Bullets. What he had heard about those brothers was scary. Jesus Perez, a tenth grader who bused tables down at Enrique's Chili and Taco place, had told him about them. "They pretty dangerous, dog. Last year there was a drive-by down the street from Central Heights. The police liked 'em for it, and they seriously wanted to take 'em down, but they never could get any proof. When I walk home from work, I cross the street if I see one of them brothers coming. I ain't looking for no trouble, and I don't want no trouble looking for me. You know what I'm saying?"

"I hear you, man," Malik had said. But the problem was he also heard Big Dee-Dee, one of his mama's girlfriends, who sometimes came over to play dominoes. "Aw, them boys get into a little trouble every change of the moon or so, but ain't nobody ever proved that they've done anything really wrong. To tell you the truth, that T-Bone boy who everybody is supposed to be scared of, my sister used to babysit him. She say he still comes over to her house every once in a while, and last year she even got him to go to a couple of services with her down at Lamb of God Church. She said during the preacher's sermon he clapped his hands and said *amen*, like he was hearing the Sermon on the Mount. Naw, them boys ain't about jack. Don't you believe everything folks around here say," Big Dee-Dee had told him as she placed down two black tiles with her sausagelike hands. Malik didn't. Still, he was bothered by Perez's words. Perez was usually down on what was happening in the neighborhood. If he said the Bullets were bad news, there was probably at least a little truth to it.

It was getting late when Malik reached his project, Central Heights. The sun was already setting in the west. In the tiny food market on the street in front of his apartment row, the fruit vendors were putting away their crisp red apples and juicy plums, already closing down for the evening. Malik opened the iron gate to his complex and searched for his apartment. They'd only moved in a couple of months ago, and all the dirty-beige units still looked pretty much the same. He opened the gate and walked across the courtyard until he came to the apartment with the familiar Snoopy-shaped tear in the screen door and the two caramel-colored Nikki Wet-Wet babies lying on the cracked concrete steps.

Malik took his backpack off and sat down on the porch. His mama would be home from her day job soon, and he had to form a strategy about the sneakers that would work on her. It wouldn't be easy. She just didn't get it, and deep down Malik had to admit that he didn't get it either. Back in the small town of Receding Lake, where they came from, it just wasn't like that. School was about school, not clothes. You didn't go to class to style. You went to learn and hopefully get a chance at a good scholarship. The name of the game was getting up and out, so the kids studied hard. Before his mama had followed her now ex-boyfriend to Houston, Malik had been a high-B student who loved biology and astronomy, and he always placed either first or second in his school's science fairs.

But now things were different. Somehow he had to come up with a way to make his mother understand that. He placed his backpack on the porch next to one of the naked dolls and tried to come up with just the right irrefutable data.

While he sat quietly working through things in his head, a tiny light brown girl with a missing front tooth and two huge Afro puffs came skipping out to the front porch. "What you doing, Malik?" she asked, picking up one of the baby dolls and sitting down beside him on the warm concrete. Malik turned to her with a big smile.

Out of all his sisters, he liked Mara the best. She was the youngest, and his mama once told him that in the Bible her name meant "bitter." But to Malik, she was like a cup of warm maple syrup and had a disposition as pleasant as fresh baby powder when you squeezed it from the plastic bottle. Somehow just seeing her pulled his spirits up. He put his arms out and pulled her into his lap.

"You know what? I made a picture in school today. It's a flower, and it's pink with yellow petals. You can have it if you want," she said.

Malik kissed her on the cheek and gently tugged her puffs. "Naw," he said. "I can't take your picture. You better hang it on your bedroom wall, where everybody can see it." He fumbled in his jean shorts pocket and yanked out an oatmeal cookie he had been saving since lunch, but before he could hand it to her, Jasmonet, his older tomboy sister, ran out on the porch and grabbed it.

"Hey!" Malik tried to grab it back, but Jasmonet just took a big bite from it.

"That was for Mara!"

"So? She don't need no cookie anyway. It'll just rot her teeth out, and ain't nobody got no money to get 'em fixed. Anyway, where you been?"

"Nowhere. I left school a little late."

"A little late. Boy, it's damn near six o'clock. School been out for at least two hours. What the heck you been doing?"

Malik didn't even try to answer her. He always lost

arguments to Jasmonet. She was cool sometimes, but mostly, she was a pain. Besides, if he told her why he was really late, she would probably just call him a punk and say that he should stand up for himself. She wouldn't understand his being afraid. She was a fighter. The first day she went to school, some older, slick-haired girl got in her face and teased her about wearing her thick kinky hair natural. Jasmonet didn't bother telling the girl that their mama couldn't afford to send her to the salon or even buy her a relaxer kit; she just balled up her fist and knocked the girl into the next zip code. She got suspended two days for fighting, but when she went back to school, nobody was fool enough to mess with her about anything.

"What the heck you been doing all this time, Malik?" Jasmonet asked him again.

"Aw, man, Jasmonet, why you always got to be tripping? I couldn't come home. Something came up, so can you please just quit sweatin' me about it?"

"Yeah, can you please quit sweatin' me about it?" Mara echoed. She stuck her tongue out at Jasmonet.

Malik laughed.

"What you laughing at?" Jasmonet yelled.

"Whatever he wants to laugh at." Malik looked up and saw their mother, an attractive middle-aged woman with short brown braids, dragging toward the porch in her yellow peasant blouse and black ruffled skirt and toting two huge bags of groceries. Malik placed Mara on the ground next to the porch and hopped down to help his mother.

"Take them groceries up there and give 'em to

Jasmonet, since she like to be in charge of everything," she said.

"Aw, Mama," Jasmonet groaned.

Malik walked up the steps, holding the bags out to his sister. "Here, big head."

"Forget you, Malik. I'ma slap you so hard, your kids gone be born with my handprint on they face!" Jasmonet yelled, taking them from him.

"And I'ma slap you so hard, you gonna do what I ask and quit working my nerves," Mama said. "Now take them bags in the house and stop showing your behind for a change. I ain't got time for no fool acting. I got to go back to work in just a few minutes."

"How come, Mama?" Malik asked, resisting the urge to stick his tongue out at his sister.

"Another bunch of foolishness. That boy Perez done run off with that pretty little fat girl who just started working a week ago, talking about getting married. Ain't neither one of them more than fifteen. They mamas and daddies was up there throwing a fit on Enrique today. He told them that he didn't know nothing about it, but he was mad as hell at Perez, 'cause it meant he had to find somebody to cover Perez's shift at the last minute. And I'm that somebody," Mama said, pulling away from Mara and sitting down on the side of the porch.

"That ain't fair, Mama," Jasmonet said.

"Well, what is, Jasmonet? 'Cause I swear I been living longer than the Israelites wandered in the desert, and I ain't figured it out yet. I sho wish somebody would do me a favor and tell me. Kids taking off, doing what they wanna do and putting the mess on other folks and they loved ones. I ain't gonna never understand that. It ain't gonna never make no sense to me. Now, go on, sweetie, and get dinner started."

"Yes, ma'am." Jasmonet kicked open the screen door with her foot and went inside.

"You go with her, Mara," Mama said, patting Mara on the bottom. "I bought you one of them toys that they giving away in the kids' meals this month. It's in the bottom of one of them bags. Run and go tell Jasmonet to give it to you."

"Yes, ma'am," Mara said, and followed her sister into the house. Malik sat back down on the porch beside his mother. He dropped his head and stared at his feet. His mother placed her arm around him.

"What's wrong, pooky? What's the matter? Why you staring at the ground like you can see clear through to the other side of the world?"

"I'm not," Malik mumbled. "I just—I was looking at my feet."

"What about 'em ?" his mother asked, leaning over to kiss him on the cheek. Malik jerked his head away.

"Aw, Mama, don't," he said.

"All right, Malik. I know you got a wrinkle in your behind somewhere. Just tell me where it is so I can get it out."

"Mama, I need some new shoes," Malik blurted out.

His mother looked down at his feet and shook her head. "I know. I guess you right. You done almost wore them down to slippers. They falling to pieces. I was praying you could hold out a little longer, but it don't look like you gonna make it. Okay, just give me a couple of weeks. When I get my next check, we'll go down to Shoe Mart and see what we can find on the discount rack."

Malik's face fell. He sighed aloud.

"What is it, pooky?" Mama asked, patting his back.

"Nothing," Malik said, not wanting to make her mad or hurt her feelings. "Nothing, Mama, it's just that . . . I can't—I can't have no more discount sneakers. I got to have what the other kids have. It's critical."

"And what do the other kids have?" his mama asked. "Look, Malik, if this is about them JC Jumper sneakers again, you can go on and hang that hat on the rack. I done told you. I got too many mouths to feed to spend two hundred bucks on some sneakers you ain't gonna want to wear but a few months. That's how silly ya'll teenage boys are. Every time ya'll see one of them basketball players selling them shoes on TV, ya'll think ya'll got to have a pair. Ya'll don't even care that it takes damn near half your mama's paycheck to pay for them."

"That's not true," Malik snapped. He had learned early not to ask for much. When he could, he made his own cash by doing odd jobs in his hood. But he just made a few dollars here and there. He never earned enough for big expenses—like shoes.

"Boy, what did you say to me?" his mama asked.

Malik flinched a little, but fortunately for him, she kept her hands to herself. "Nothing, I'm sorry. It's just . . . Look, Mama, you don't get it. I'm not trying to be about wearing something because everybody else got it. I'm not even like that, and you know it. I just, Mama, I really need those sneakers. It's imperative that I have them. You don't understand. I got to have them or else."

"Or else what? What do you mean by that? And don't be using none of them big words like *im-per-a-tive* with me. I told you to save all them fancy words for your science classes."

"I know, I'm sorry. I don't know what to tell you, Mama. I just got to have 'em."

"And folks in hell got to have ice water, too," his mama said sharply, but then her voice turned pillow-soft. She reached over and gently placed her hand under his chin. "Look at me, Malik."

Malik looked up at her. He felt shame when he saw the sadness clouding her eyes, even more shame than he felt each time he ran from the other boys.

"Look, Malik. I know it's been hard on you and your sisters, and I know that ya'll done had to do without a lot of things because of some of my decisions."

"It's okay, Mama."

"Naw, no it ain't. Malik, I'd wrap every damn sneaker up in the world in colored tissue paper and give 'em to you and your sisters if I could," Mama said, caressing his cheek. "I'd give ya'll everything that you see them other kids out in the street with, 'cause ya'll the reason why I ask the Lord to wake me up each morning, but I can't. I love you and your sisters, but God molded me from dust, not platinum. What you see is what you get. I just can't give you what I don't have. I know some of them other mamas put them shoes on the layaway and pay 'em off that way, but I can't even afford to do that. Now, to use one of your fancy words, you good at theorizing about stuff. How you the-o-rize we gonna eat with you wearing the food money on your feet? I'm sorry, I know you don't think it's fair, but just like I told Jasmonet, I been living over four decades and I ain't seen much that is. You just gonna have to take them discount shoes and make do."

"Okay, Mama," Malik mumbled.

His mama leaned over and kissed him. "I gotta run, pudding. I'll see you when I get home tonight," she said, struggling up from the porch. "Ooh, Lord, I'm tired. I hope we ain't too busy tonight."

"Me, too, Mama," Malik said. He put his arm around her waist and walked her back up the walkway. His mother kissed him again, and Malik stood on the sidewalk and waved to her until she was several blocks away. When he saw her cross the project parking lot, he returned to the porch to think. He had struck out with his mama for the final time and even pissed her off by using words that he usually knew he should keep to himself. What on earth was he going to do now?

Day bled into night. The sun and moon exchanged places. The streetlamps flickered on, bathing the neighborhood in hazy yellow light, but Malik didn't notice. He was deep in thought. He had felt awful when he saw how distressed his mama was about the sneakers, but now he wasn't sure why he had even felt that way.

The truth was, his mama had made a mess out of all of their lives. She was a good woman, but she had problems finding good men. The guys she hooked up with weren't total losers. A couple of them were really nice. But when it came to commitment, they skipped right over that track on the CD. The dudes just didn't know how to settle down, and each time one of them left, he took all the cash he could find in her panty drawer and every piece of furniture he had added to the house. The only thing he left her with was a watermelon belly and a promise that pretty soon her grocery store list was going to include the word *diapers*. It was what his mama seemed to do best, create new life—and make life harder for the kids she already had hanging around.

He loved her, but what right did she have to do that? It wasn't fair. Mama always made crappy decisions and thought everybody else ought to live with them. Why should he have to do without? He kept saying that to himself, as if someone or something deep inside him would suddenly shout out an answer. Was he wrong to want the boys off his back? Was he wrong to want the sneakers that all the other kids had? He didn't think so. He flung his backpack through the hole in the screen door and left the apartment to find Sandra's.

Malik had taken less time deciding to go to Sandra's than he had deciding to do his last science project on the rings of Saturn, but when he made it to the lounge, he hesitated. Inside the old limestone building with the blacked-out windows might be some major bad dudes. And even the rusting metal welcome sign, with laughing sexy Sandra, in her skintight black dress and two-inch high heels, didn't make him want to rush inside. He had no idea what the real outcome would be if he chose to go through the door, and he usually didn't like doing anything without even a small working hypothesis. Still, Carl had told him that the Bullets could help him out. It had to be worth the risk of hanging with them for a little while.

He walked up to the heavy wooden door and rapped on it hard. The minute hand on his watch went around three full cycles, and all he heard was the occasional roar of a car rolling down the street in front of the club. He was about to rap on the door again when it sprang open. Cautiously, he walked inside.

Brightness. That was what struck him as he entered the lounge. The large square space was completely lit by long fluorescent ceiling lamps just like the ones in his classrooms at school. Malik didn't know what to make of it, nor did he know what to make of what he saw. Towering oak bookcases loaded with paper- and hardback volumes sat against each of the four walls. Malik recognized the names of some of the authors from his English class. Richard Wright, Mark Twain, John Steinbeck, Nikki Giovanni, William Faulkner, Zora Neale Hurston, and James Baldwin. He had read at least one story or poem by each of them, but there were many others that he hadn't read, so many that Malik wondered if he hadn't stumbled into a library by accident. He considered backing out of the room and rechecking the sign on the door. The tapping sound of footprints on the hardwood floor behind him stopped him from leaving.

He turned to see Carl and another boy approaching him. The boy looked like he could be a couple of years older than Carl, and he was huge like him. He was built up like a pro wrestler or linebacker. And he was fly, decked out in a dark gray suit with a wine-colored tie and sharp maroon Stacy Adams shoes. His head was shaved completely bald. Intelligent and serious eyes peered out from behind round plastic-framed black glasses. He looked like either a preacher or a professor, Malik didn't know which.

"Hey, what's up, dog?" Carl asked, walking over to him with a huge grin.

"N-N-Nothing," Malik stuttered. "I just thought I would come over and hang, like you said I could."

"Good, that's cool," Carl said, placing his arm around Malik's shoulder. "I'm glad you showed up, little bro. I was just telling T-Bone about you."

"T-Bone?" Malik said with a shocked look on his face. In his Sunday suit the other boy looked more like a Michael or a Joshua. Malik wondered if he got his name because he liked to eat steak.

"That's right, I'm T-Bone, young brother," the well-dressed boy said, extending his hand to Malik for a traditional handshake. He had a concrete grip. Malik wriggled free and began rubbing his knuckles.

"I'm sorry, little bro, but they say a firm handshake is the testimony of a man's character," T-Bone said. "I see you've been checking out my book collection. Are you an avid reader?"

"I read some, mostly science books, but I kinda like Richard Wright," Malik lied, pointing to a copy of *Native Son*.

"An excellent choice; the struggle of an African-American male in an oppressive world. It's Black Nationalist Literature, meant to effect a change," T-Bone said, walking over to the shelf and touching the copy.

"I guess," Malik said, not really knowing what the heck Black Nationalist meant and trying to recall the book from his advanced English studies session.

Carl patted him on the back. "Don't let T-Bone mess with your head too much, Malik. He just talking about brothers letting other folks know that we don't like being pushed around. His grandfather was one of them lawyers or something, back in the day when black folks ain't had no rights. He likes to read all them fancy books and talk all complicated, but he's down like the rest of us. And I already told him about your problem. He knew you would be stopping by."

"Oh, yes, JC Jumpers," T-Bone said, looking at Malik's sneakers and shaking his head. "Your footwear is in pitiful condition, little brother. My grandfather was a lawyer, but my father washes dishes at a hotel downtown. I know how it is to get beat down everyday because your shoes and clothing keep you out of the game. It's why I told Carl he could tell you to come."

"Thanks," Malik said, beginning to feel just a bit more at ease. He still thought T-Bone was a little strange. But T-Bone had already brought up the sneakers without his having to mention them. That made T-Bone pretty cool.

"Come with me," T-Bone said, walking to a door at the end of the long room and opening it.

Inside the door was a small room that made more sense to Malik. Sitting in a corner of the room was a black lacquer entertainment center complete with a big-screen TV and a brand-new Xbox. And if that wasn't fantastic enough, in front of the TV was a plush three-piece sectional sofa with plenty of room to stretch out on. Malik wanted to run to the sofa and flip on the tube, but sitting there thumbing through copies of *Vibe* and *Jet* magazines were two other boys Malik hadn't yet spotted around his hood. Even lounging, Malik could tell that one of the boys, with his kinky hair shaved around the sides and dyed cherry-Twizzler red on the top, had to be a Goliath. His legs were longer than the cornstalks that used to grow in the field across from Malik's backyard, and his riverboat feet had to be sporting at least a size 15 pair of leather JC Jumper sneakers.

The second boy on the sofa shot him a quick glance out of the corner of his eye. Malik noticed that the boy was much smaller than his three friends, but still buff. He was handsome, too, almost to the point of being feminine.

"Skillet, Orlando, put those magazines away and come

say hello to Malik," T-Bone said in a commanding voice. The boys hopped up immediately and hurried over to him. Malik stuck out his hand for shakes.

"I'm Skillet. What's up, dog?" the Goliath boy asked, pumping his hand up and down in the traditional style as well.

"The brother needs some shoes, that's what's up," Carl said just as Skillet pulled his hand away.

"Damn, man," the second boy said, glancing down at Malik's feet as he stuck out his hand, too. "Them shoes look like you done left them on the tracks and somebody done run 'em over with a train." All the boys belly laughed. Malik wanted to fall into a black hole.

"Aw, man, don't be like that," the second boy said, noticing his face. "I'm Orlando, and when I was little, my mama used to be so broke, she didn't have enough money to get me a decent haircut. She used to pull my hair back with a scrunchie or braid it all up. When I walked in the schoolroom, everybody would be laughing at me and saying I looked like a girl. It made me feel like a old mangy dog that somebody done kicked all in the butt."

"I know what you mean," Carl said. "You got to live it—to get it."

"You ain't lying, man," all the boys said at the same time.

Malik beamed. The boys weren't frontin'. They knew what it felt like to have to do without. They had literally walked in the same raggedy sneakers as him. Why had he been afraid to come and hang out with them? He saw no evidence that they were thugs or gangsters. Except for T-Bone, they were all dressed in nice jeans and either a blue or white T-shirt with a red Tommy Hilfiger logo on the sleeve. Their hair wasn't wrapped in doo-rags, and he didn't see any weed or tattoos on their upper arms or necks. So far nobody had offered him a bar to drag on or crack rock to stick in a pipe, and the only hoochie in the club was a black-and-white painting of sexy Sandra in her skintight dress hanging on the wall behind the entertainment center. Malik thought back to what Perez had said about the guys. What the heck did Perez know? He'd run off with some stupid girl he barely knew and caused trouble for himself and everyone else he knew.

"I'm glad I came to hang with you guys," Malik said.

"Good," Carl said. He walked over to the TV and turned it off. "Tomorrow you won't go to school all tore up."

"No, he won't," T-Bone said. "Let's go get the man what he came here for."

And just like that, the boys were off.

As they left Sandra's, Malik floated on a bed of cumulus clouds. All he could think of was how good he was going to look in his new sneakers. He was gonna be off the hook, maybe even cooler than Jordan and Shaq, and definitely cooler than Jamar and his crew. His sneaks would be even newer, brand-new from the local mall—at least he assumed they would be. Where the shoes would come from was unnecessary data to him, like how long it would take to bail the water from a sinking rowboat when you didn't have a bucket anyway. He simply wanted to know that everything was going to be just fine, and his instincts told him it was.

As he walked beside the boys, rapping with them about their favorite video games and books, he ran off the one remaining thing that bothered him about the group: their name. He decided that they had chosen a name like the Bullets because it was just a way of keeping the other boys out of their face. It sounded powerful, strong, downright hard-core. Nobody would ever think that they were just a group of guys who liked to do a lot of regular stuff. It was just plain ole survival, and Malik understood survival. It was what he had been doing for thirteen years.

"Say, Malik, what size shoe you wear?" Carl asked as they cut across a vacant parking lot.

"Ten," Malik said, glad that at least his feet were average size.

"Okay, if that's what you need, that's what you'll have," T-Bone said.

"Thanks, man," Malik said with a big grin. He was happier than the first time he got to see plant cells through a microscope.

A few vacant lots, blocks, and a fried-chicken stand later, the boys stopped. They tossed their soiled chicken bags filled with gnawed bones into a rain gutter and walked into what Malik was certain was the back of the playground at the Lamb of God Church. Malik grew irritated. What were they doing here? Had the boys changed their minds about his sneakers and suddenly decided they wanted to go to a church service? Shoot, he needed sneakers, not prayer. If he thought prayer would have gotten him the sneakers, he would have been on his knees every morning and night for the past few weeks. Naw, what he needed was a trip to Foot Locker or Champs. Why were the boys wasting time doing this? Why were they just standing behind the tall shrubs?

"Hey, Carl, what we doing here, man? I thought we were gonna get some sneaks?" Malik said, getting as far away from the pointy foliage as he could.

"We are," Carl whispered back, standing next to him in the freshly cut grass. "Just hold up and chill for a minute. Don't make so much noise."

"How come?"

"Silence," T-Bone quietly commanded from a few steps in front of them. He was positioned right near the bushes, his huge head moving from side to side as if he was trying to see through the small holes between the leaves. Everyone, including Malik, clammed up. They got so quiet that Malik could actually hear the church's new Colors of America flag flapping softly on the front-yard flagpole. And that wasn't all. On the other side of the high bushes he could also hear the familiar *whap* and *swish* of a basketball bouncing against the blacktop and falling through a rope net.

Somebody was shooting hoops on the court.

Malik eased up next to T-Bone and peered between the bushes. In the dim glow of an overhead court light he could see an average-size boy about Jasmonet's age dribbling a ball and throwing it through the net with hardly any effort at all. The ball just seemed to glide from his hand and into the net.

"Let's go," T-Bone whispered.

The boys walked out to the court as quietly as sugar ants crawling up a picnic basket. They strolled over to the basketball player and stood behind his back, uttering no sound, making no movement. The player dribbled the ball and ran to the net for a dunk. Malik watched in astonishment as he gracefully sprang from the ground and tossed the shot in. The ball hit the concrete and bounced back to the player. He flew up to the net again for another elegant dunk.

Wow, Malik said to himself as the player threw the ball in. It whooshed through the net and bounced on the court in front of T-Bone. The boy dashed over to retrieve it.

"You're pretty good," T-Bone spoke up as the player scooped the ball up and began dribbling it. The player glanced at T-Bone and the rest of the boys curiously.

"I guess," he said. He ran back to the net and tossed the ball in.

"Play much, bro?" Skillet asked as the ball whooshed through the net and hit the court again.

"Yeah, pretty much. I'm a center over at Bethune," the player said, chasing after the ball. T-Bone reached out and grabbed it. The player stopped. "Say, bro, toss me the ball," the player said, reaching toward T-Bone.

"What, this ball?" T-bone asked, holding the ball up and spinning it on his oversized finger.

"Yeah, that ball," the player said with a chuckle. "It's getting late, and a brother is hungry. I gotta finish my practice, so I can go have some of my mama's brown-sugar spareribs."

"Brown-sugar spareribs, sounds tasty, but I'd actually like to hold on to this ball for a while. I kind of like it," T-Bone said with a straight face. "The last ball I owned was one of those rubber foam balls, when I was a lot younger. This ball is much better."

"Yeah, I had one of those foam balls, too, when I was a kid." The player laughed. "Me and my little pickle-head brother used to fight over it all the time, until my pops finally bought us the real thing."

"Did your pops buy you that one?" Skillet asked, cutting his eyes at T-Bone.

"Sure, he just got it for my birthday last month. He said the better the ball, the better the player. I don't know if that's true, but you know how it is when your old man is trying to help you out. Hand it over, dog. I got to go," the player said, reaching for the ball again. T-Bone didn't move.

"Naw, I don't know how it is when your old man is trying to help you out." Orlando spoke up now, smoothing down a wave in his raven hair. "It must be nice. My daddy ain't never helped me out with nothing. He ain't never gave me jack, not even his sorry-ass last name. Imagine that, imagine a father not wanting to sign up on his own flesh and blood."

"I can't imagine," the player said, looking confused, and this time he didn't grin.

"Naw, I guess you can't imagine," Orlando said, checking out the yellow FUBU label going down the side of the boy's red muscle shirt and shorts. "I don't believe you can imagine at all. You don't look like you hurting for nothing."

"He's not, so of course he can't imagine. He doesn't know the struggle," T-Bone said, rolling his eyes at the boy. "He's a pampered flower. The anti-ghetto boy."

"The anti-what? What are you talking about?"

"Ghetto boy, you're different. Left out of the loop. I can tell just by looking at you. And, oh yes, really nice shoes," T-Bone said, looking at the boy's feet.

Malik looked at the boy's feet, too. Man, T-Bone was right. He definitely wasn't a kid who knew about doing without. Malik had seen those leather-and-suede high-tops in a hip-hop mag last month. They were the top-of-the-line JC Jumpers, a cool three hundred bucks on sale. Malik got completely green inside. The truth was, he was just like Orlando. He had his mother's last name, and he hadn't seen his old man since he was nine.

"Well, your daddy must really think you all that," Malik said sarcastically to the player.

The boy shrugged. "I guess. I don't even know what ya'll talking about. Just give me my ball, man, and I'ma roll on home. Ya'll tripping on something. Anti-ghetto. I can't even understand all that."

"I know you can't," T-Bone said, staring at the player

icily, casually passing the ball from hand to hand. "I know you don't get it. It's impossible for somebody like you to comprehend. Clearly you have more skills than sense, but I suppose somebody like you wouldn't really need much of that."

"What? Look, dog, you don't even know me like that. So I ain't even thinking about you, fool. All of ya'll ain't talking nothing but nonsense, so just give me my stuff, and I'll see ya'll never," the player said, grabbing for the ball.

T-Bone stepped back with it. "No. Like I said, I kind of like this ball," he said coldly, while still passing the ball from one hand to another. "I think I'll keep it a little while longer. That's not a problem for you, is it?"

"Hell yeah, that's a—" the player started to say, but the words jammed in his throat. He dropped his hands to his sides, and his dark pupils moved rapidly over T-Bone's bulging muscles and his giant rugged hands, hands that looked like they could squeeze the air from a basketball—or a neck. His grin returned, but this time it was fake, forced. "Hey, you know what? Go on and take the ball, bro. It ain't nothing but a thing. I don't even know why I was trying to get it back from you."

"Thanks, man. I knew you would understand how I felt about it," T-Bone said, glaring at the player from behind his black-framed glasses. The boy nodded and backed away farther, his eyes still fixed on T-Bone's hands.

Malik started to get seriously unnerved. The discomfort in him went through an uneasy mitosis, separating itself into fear and guilt. He focused on the ugly game that he knew T-Bone was playing with the boy. Plain and simple, it wasn't right. It was cruel and seemed beneath the intelligent T-Bone he had met just a few hours earlier. The things Perez had said about the Bullets folded themselves back into Malik's brain. *"I cross the street if I see one of them brothers coming."* Malik hated to admit it, but he was beginning to see why.

"Carl, this ain't right," Malik whispered. "We should give him back his stuff and let him go on about his business. I thought we were going to get some sneakers. Why are we standing around doing this?"

"Malik, just be cool. You about to make a mess out of everything," Carl said, turning to him with annoyance all over his scarred face. Malik got quiet again. He didn't dare ask what he was making a mess out of.

"What, you don't want your ball back?" T-Bone taunted the player.

The boy shook his head vigorously. "Naw, keep it. I got plenty," he said, backing away even more.

"Where you going, man? You got someplace you need to be?" Skillet walked up and got in front of the player. He was inches from the boy's face and nearly a full head taller. "You got some more balls at home?" Skillet laughed. "I guess you do, 'cause it sho don't look like you got none here. Just look at your legs. Why you trembling, man? Ain't nobody doing nothing to you."

Malik glanced at the player's legs. It looked like there

was an earthquake going on beneath his feet. Malik felt sorry for him. He knew what it felt like to have wobbly limbs.

"Aw, man, I'm just playing with you," Skillet said, reaching out like he was going to give the boy a playful pat on the cheek. The player ducked away.

"Damn, you scary," Orlando said. "Go on and get outta here, man. We just messing with you. Go be with your mama."

"Okay, for real?" the player asked.

"Of course. You said you had to go eat dinner. Go have a nice supper," T-Bone said.

"Okay," the player said, stepping cautiously around Skillet. Skillet moved to let him by. The boy started off the court, and Malik breathed a sigh of relief. It looked like everything was over. Maybe T-Bone and the other boys were just funnin' with the player, like Skillet said. Malik was willing to believe that until he noticed that T-Bone still had the boy's ball, was still tossing it from hand to hand. Why hadn't he given it back?

Malik swallowed hard. He watched the player walking shakily away from the court and wished the boy would quicken his pace. The player reached the edge of the blacktop and whipped around to see if anyone was following him.

Bam! T-Bone slammed the ball against the side of the player's face. The player stumbled, nearly tripping over his own ball as it fell to the court. A second later Skillet and Orlando were all over him. They dragged him, struggling and dizzy, back to T-Bone, his JC Jumpers scraping the blacktop.

"Say, man, what's wrong with ya'll? Let me go. I ain't done nothing to ya'll!" the player yelled.

"Really, I think you have," T-Bone spat, as Orlando and Skillet pulled the boy in front of him.

"No, I ain't. I don't know what you're talking about," the player cried. His eyes were now giant with fright. "I don't even know ya'll, man! What ya'll want with me?"

T-Bone swiped the player's legs from beneath him. He fell backward, landing with a hard thud on his butt.

"That's 'What do you all want with me?'" T-Bone corrected, like an angry schoolteacher. "A young man like you should know better. Star athlete, daddy's favorite—surely your father has taught you the importance of speaking proper English."

"What—What English?" the boy stammered. "I don't know what you talking about. Just leave me alone, and let me go on about my business."

"Aw, shut up, fool!" Skillet shouted. "Just shut up. You already done got on my last nerve. Quit acting like a little punk. Ain't nobody even hardly touched you yet." He grabbed the player by his collar and yanked him to his tiptoes. "You know why they call me Skillet?" he asked.

The boy opened his mouth, but no sound came out.

"They call me Skillet 'cause I fry up little pampered-ass punks like you for dinner. That's right. You ain't nothing to me, you or your pops," Skillet said, twisting the player's shirt.

The boy started gasping. "Let me go, man, please," he pleaded in a raspy voice, trying to pry Skillet's fingers off of his collar. Skillet let the boy go, and he fell back onto the blacktop.

"Punk!" Skillet cried.

"What's—What's wrong with you, man?" the player asked, panting.

That's what Malik wanted to know. He had seen bullying before, but this was something else. Hatred. It was suddenly there standing in the midst of them. Malik could see it reflected in all the other boys' faces. He didn't get it. What was up with T-Bone and the Bullets? As far as he knew, the Bullets had no reason at all to be angry with this kid they didn't even know.

"Don't be asking me what's wrong with me. What's wrong with you? Punks like you make me sick," Skillet said, and spat a huge wad next to the boy's leg.

"What did I do, man?" the player asked, moving as far away as he could from the expanding blob. "What's wrong with ya'll? Just tell me what I did."

"What do you think you've done?" T-Bone said, leaning over the player. The boy began frantically scooting in the other direction.

"I ain't done nothing. I was just out here shooting some hoops!" he shouted.

"I know. You're out here every night, every night just throwing that ball up in the air, so you can get better, so you can be the man," T-Bone said, slapping the player hard on the leg. "When you go to school, boys gather around you like first graders around an ice-cream truck. They want to get some of what you have. You like that, don't you? It makes you feel good. You can decide who gets to do layups on your court. The lucky ones get to play for a couple of quarters. The unlucky ones don't even get to sit on the bench. Isn't that right?"

"Answer him!" Skillet said. He bent down and back-handed the boy across the face.

The boy yelled, and tears begin to rush down his dark cheeks. "I don't know what you talking about," he whimpered. "Ya'll must be crazy."

T-Bone pointed at the player's face. "No, we're not crazy. And you do know what I'm talking about, so stop pretending. What I'm speaking about is all the boys that you think you're better than because your father buys you things. I'm speaking about boys like me—and my little brother, Malik. Malik! Get over here."

Malik stayed put. Whatever this was, he wanted no part of it.

"Carl, this ain't right. Why they messing with him? I don't want to go over there," he whispered. But when Carl turned to him, he saw that Carl had the same look on his face as T-Bone, Orlando, and Skillet. He looked like he could tear the player's head off and hurl it through the basketball net.

Malik shuddered.

"Come on!" T-Bone shouted. "Come over here, Malik, and face your fear."

Malik didn't move. Orlando stepped away from the

boy, grabbed Malik by the arm, and began dragging him toward T-Bone. Malik wanted to struggle, but he was too afraid. Resisting certainly hadn't done the player any good. He didn't want these guys mad at him, too. He allowed Skillet to pull him over to the drama. Skillet let him go, and T-Bone pointed to the boy.

"Look at him," he said. "Look at what you've been afraid of for months. Is he scary now? Is he something to run away from or envy? Just look at him. He's nothing but a coward, crying over a little slap. Even his sharp basketball skills and expensive clothes can't hide what he is. Just look at him, Malik."

Malik forced himself to look down at the sobbing player. The boy's cheeks were streaked with wetness. A large dark bruise had already formed on the side of his face where T-Bone had struck him with the ball, and a small trickle of blood had gathered in the corner of his mouth where Skillet had slapped him.

T-Bone kicked the boy's leg savagely, and the boy screamed in pain. "See? I told you, nothing but a mama's boy."

"I ain't no mama's boy!" the boy yelled back, rubbing his leg.

"Shut up, fool," Skillet said, hitting him directly in the mouth this time. Malik watched the red liquid drip down the player's jaw and felt sick.

"Forget you, man!" the boy cried, wiping the side of his mouth. He was obviously tapping into some hidden courage.

"What did you say, punk? You better be quiet, fool, and stop wearing on my nerves, 'cause I got something in my pocket that will shut you up for good," Skillet said, reaching into his jeans. His hand emerged with what looked like a closed switchblade. Malik turned into a statue with fear, but before Skillet could go after the boy with the blade, T-Bone caught his arm.

"Put that away. It's not necessary," he said. "He can scream like a little girl all he wants, but there's nothing he can do. This time *we* get to make the choices."

"Yeah, that's true, man," Skillet said, nodding his head and pushing the blade back in his pocket. Malik breathed a sigh of relief. He didn't want to see the player cut, and he certainly didn't want to be a part of any stabbing. What would his family think? His family . . . the girls had probably eaten dinner by now and were sitting down to watch their favorite TV show or play cards. He wished he were there. He wished he had just followed Jasmonet into the house and helped her cook.

"Of course it's true," T-Bone said to Skillet. He bent down and tried to yank one of the boy's shoes off. The boy kicked his feet wildly, but T-bone was still able to grasp him by the leg. He jerked the sneaker free, tossed it to Carl, and then yanked the second sneaker off and did the same with it.

Carl checked out the tag in the tongue. "Eleven. He'll have to put on a couple of pairs of thick socks, but they'll suit a little brother just right."

Carl walked over and handed the shoes out to Malik.

"Here you go, homey," he said with a huge grin. "You gonna have the best shoes in the schoolyard."

Malik's jaw fell to the blacktop. The reality of what was really going on dropped out of the sky like a fiery comet and landed right in front of his face. When the smoke cleared, he felt sicker than he had ever felt in his life. All this time he hadn't suspected it at all, didn't even see it coming. He looked at the pricey sneakers and wished that he had no feet. What had he done? Was he the cause of all of this madness? He was smart; how could he not have at least suspected that this was where the Bullets were getting their fly threads from? "I don't want them," he said. "Give 'em back."

"What? Don't be a fool, Malik!" T-Bone yelled. He snatched the shoes from Carl and shoved them directly into Malik's face. The sweaty smell of the player's insoles made Malik want to gag.

"What's the matter with you? You said you wanted new shoes, and we got them for you. Take them," T-Bone growled, wild-eyed. "Don't be a complete idiot."

Malik shook his head violently. "I don't want them. I changed my mind. Just give 'em back to him," he pleaded, backing away. "This ain't right. He ain't done nothing to us. We don't have a right to take his things."

"Of course we do," T-Bone spat, shoving the shoes harder into Malik's chest with his gigantic dark hands. "Look at him. Look who he is, what he is. It's about effecting a change. That's what my grandfather used to say. He used to say that sometimes you have to do something drastic to make your feelings heard. We're making our feelings known. We're taking back what brothers like him have taken away from us. He's not a bully like Jamar, but he's the same thing. He's just another punk keeping guys like me and you out. We don't mean anything to him. Don't you get that?"

"I don't know what you're talking about. He never did anything to me. Just give him back his stuff," Malik said honestly. He glanced over at the church's darkened stained-glass windows and wished the heavyset sexton who normally patrolled the grounds were on duty. He was as big as T-Bone and Carl, and he looked like he could give hell to a group of pit bulls. He would have run all of them off before any of this got started.

"Malik, he don't need these shoes. He'll be all right. His daddy will get him some more," Carl said in his usual big-brother tone, and for a second Malik wanted to do what he asked. Only he knew better. You didn't make your soup richer by taking the meat from someone else's pot. He understood that. No matter how needy his family had gotten in the past, they had never pulled themselves up by yanking another person down. He shook his head again.

"Naw, Carl, I can't do that."

"But, Malik—" Carl began. T-Bone cut him off.

"Don't beg him," he said in a suddenly calm voice. "If he doesn't want them, he doesn't want them." He took the shoes from Carl and flung them into the bushes. "*Malik* doesn't have to take anything from the boy," he said. "No, he doesn't have to take anything at all." He turned back to Skillet and Orlando and nodded his head. To Malik's horror, the two boys pounced on the player and began grabbing at his outfit.

"Get off of me, leave me alone," the player screamed as his muscle shirt and shorts began ripping away.

"Hey, leave him alone!" Malik cried, trying to get around T-Bone. T-Bone pushed him to the ground. An intense pain shot through him. He lay there for a few seconds holding his back. When he finally struggled to his feet, he saw that the player was completely stripped down to nothing but a pair of ragged white cotton briefs. His designer shirt and shorts lay in tatters at his feet. He was bawling now, shaking hard with his arms wrapped tightly around his knees.

"Look at him, Malik!" T-Bone raged with his fists balled up. "I told you. On the outside he's a van Gogh, but underneath he's nothing but a cheap knockoff poster. You're a fool for not taking his shoes. He doesn't deserve them. Carl told me that you were really smart. Why are you being so dumb? Answer me!"

Malik stuffed the cotton in his ears, like he did with Jasmonet, so he could hear his own thoughts. In his head he formed a strategy. Quickly, he broke away from the group and raced to the player's fallen basketball. He picked it up and threw it as hard as he could into the Bullets. Instinctively, they moved to dodge the ball. While they were caught off guard, the basketball player scrambled to his feet. He stumbled once but managed to sprint past Malik and into the bushes. Malik wasted no time following his lead.

"Hey, that fool is getting away," he heard Skillet yell as he pushed through the foliage and into the street. "Let's go get 'im."

"Yeah, man, let's go," Orlando echoed.

"No, leave him. He's just a pathetic little punk anyway. Let him go," he heard T-Bone yell back at the other two boys. Malik didn't know if the Bullets were talking about him or the basketball player, but it didn't matter. He was small and fast. He ran and ran until pieces of his torn soles started to break off and he was completely out of breath. When he stopped, he was several blocks away from the playground. He turned and looked behind him, but all he saw was a long dark vacant street. Panting hard, he made his way back to his home, thinking about what had just happened. How could he have been so stupid? When he did science experiments, he never ignored warnings. If his teachers told him something was dangerous, he believed them, and yet he hadn't believed any of the bad things that he heard about the Bullets. He had gotten himself into a huge mess, and all he had to show for it was more trouble. Tomorrow, when the darkness faded into light again, he would still be running without a doubt from Jamar and his crew, and now maybe even from crazy T-Bone and the Bullets. Malik felt scared and upset with himself about that, but what really bothered him was that a tiny part of him was beginning to think that maybe he should have taken the shoes. He thought about them lying new and barely used in the bushes where T-Bone had flung them. It didn't seem logical to just leave them there. It would be a waste, and his mama had taught him to never throw away anything that he could make good use of. Maybe when he got home from school tomorrow he would go and see if they were still there . . . just maybe.

Back in the day, I was a kid much like Malik. I grew up in the hood. I was the youngest of four siblings, and my parents never had the cash to buy me the in-style gear. I wore mostly cheap hand-me-downs and dresses that my mother could whip up on her Singer sewing machine. I remember getting my butt kicked a lot because of it.

I guess in many ways I wrote this story for me—and for all the other kids who have gone through what I went through. I wanted to write a story that examined the "fitting in" issue from both sides: the kids who get ostracized and abused simply because they don't look or act like everyone else, and the bullies who mistreat them because of it. This is kind of a complex story that won't yield any easy answers, but I think readers will come away from it with a better understanding of how it feels to be the kid on the outs.

Lori Aurelia Williams

Lori Aurelia Williams received the PEN/Phyllis Naylor Working Writer Fellowship for a work in progress. She also holds a master's degree in English from the University of Texas, where she was awarded a James Michener Fellowship in creative writing. Her fiction is set in her hometown of Houston, Texas, and combines African-American storytelling with street slang. Her first novel, *When Kambia Elaine Flew in from Neptune*, was selected as a Best Book for Young Adults by the American Library Association, and a Best Young Adult Book of 2001 from the Texas Institute of Letters, and it was nominated for a book award by the *Los Angeles Times* and *Teen People* magazine. Her second book is *Shayla's Double-Brown Baby Blues*. She is currently at work on her third novel.

Picky Eater

Stephen Roos

I

He looks at the yellow glop on his plate and shakes his head in despair. "It's macaroni and cheese," his mom tells him.

"I know what it is, Mom. That's not the issue."

"You're not going to eat it?"

"It's bad enough looking at that glop."

When he looks up, he sees her shaking her head at him. She's where his alert blue eyes and slightly pointy chin come from. As usual, she's wearing her sweats.

He picks up his plate and carries it to the big black plastic bag lying under the sink.

"You better not be throwing out good food, Woody!"

"You're calling this food?" he asks, scraping the glop into the garbage. "It's what we had for lunch at school, Mom!"

"Cafeteria food is not the end of the world," she points out. "People do worse, Woody."

He's got his hand on the door. "I'm going out, Mom."

"You be back in time to do my checkbook," she tells him. "You promised, Woody."

She takes another forkful of the glop. As she swallows it, she turns to him. "Yum!" she says, flashing a big smile in his direction.

He opens the kitchen door and stomps down the back steps. It's September and the wind off the lake is cold. He should have grabbed a sweater, but he's in no mood to face his mother again right away.

Next door is the Hirsts'. Like Woody and his mom, they live in Kismet all year round. Their bungalow is blue. Woody's is red. The backyards are minuscule. Barely enough room for a patch of lawn, a barbecue, and some lawn furniture, which Woody was supposed to fold up and put in the shed, which is painted red to match the house.

The little dock isn't safe, but Woody walks out on it anyway. There used to be a little outboard tied up there, but Woody's brother took it when he moved out. Just before the sun sets, the glare on the water gets really bad. Woody shields his eyes as he looks across the water. He sees a fresh heap of blue wood directly across the lake. They've torn down another bungalow.

"It's called 'gentrification,' Woody. It's coming closer every day. I hear someone made an offer for the Bradys' house."

As the boy turns, he sees old Mr. Hirst from next door.

As per usual, he's dragging the oxygen tank behind him in what used to be the trolley for his golf bag. There's a plastic tube that goes from the tank right up Mr. Hirst's nose.

"Gentrification? What's that?"

"It's when rich people move in and force the poor people out."

Woody nods. He knows what's going on. He just hasn't heard that word before. "They pay a lot," Woody says. "That's what my brother told me."

Mr. Hirst shrugs. "I guess. You hungry yet, Woody?"

"It's not like I'm starving," he assures Mr. Hirst.

"Mrs. Hirst's making tuna salad. There's more than enough, Woody. I figure with school starting back up and your mom working in the cafeteria . . ."

Woody smiles. It's the first time he's gone sponging since school let out last spring, but people around here know him and his mom pretty well. But tuna salad? He could do worse, but why settle when he might find something more to his liking? "I guess I'm not that hungry after all."

"Well, if you change your mind, Woody," Mr. Hirst says.

Woody watches the old man turn and start dragging his oxygen tank back to the house. He's practically at the house when Woody starts running after him. "Mr. Hirst?" Woody calls out.

"Yes, Woody?"

"What are you guys having for dessert?"

"Cobbler," Mr. Hirst says. "Mrs. Hirst made it this afternoon. The last of her peaches from her tree."

"Maybe I'll drop by later, Mr. Hirst."

"That'd be nice, Woody."

He waits till he hears the door slam. Turning his back on the lake, he walks through the neighborhood. It's mostly bungalows where he lives. Different colors but otherwise identical. One floor. Slightly pitched roofs. Small lots. Now that summer's over, most of them are empty. He likes checking out other people's houses. It's best this time of year, when the people aren't home.

What he likes best is the quiet. There's no motorboats out on the water. There's no little kids screaming on the beach. No teenagers hanging out at the hot-dog stand, playing their music so loud, you could burst your eardrums. Woody is a teenager now. He was thirteen in February. But so far, it's more like a technicality than something real. He just doesn't feel like a teenager yet.

As he turns the next corner, the sun sets. It's twilight now all around him. All he hears is wind in the trees, making the leaves flap. Woody stands still, letting the wind and the twilight seal him off from the world, making him safe and alone.

The Grillos' house is two houses down from the water. It's the only house with a light on inside. Nelson's out back of his house. He's in the same grade as Woody. At school, they never talk, don't even nod when they pass each other in the hall. When none of the kids are around, it's okay for them to hang out.

Nelson's spinning around too fast to notice Woody. He's wearing a pink T-shirt and a skirt, also pink. The faster he spins, the higher the skirt floats up. It's forming a right angle with his body. Underneath he's got on yellow underpants. They're shiny, too, or Woody wouldn't see them in the dusk.

With both hands, Nelson twirls a baton in a little circle around his head. It's got a pink tassel at one end and a yellow tassel at the other end. The underpants, Woody realizes now, are part of the costume.

"Two, four, six, eight!" Nelson chants. "Kismet's team will be your fate!"

He flings the baton into the air. When it begins its descent, it's clear that it's going to land a lot closer to Woody than to Nelson.

"I got it!" Woody yells.

But when he makes a grab for it, he fumbles it and the baton lands on the grass.

"I could have caught it myself, you know." Nelson scowls as he picks it up. Even when he scowls, though, his face is bland, harmless. His shoulders are so narrow, you'd almost think his arms were growing out of his neck.

"You think you're going to make the squad?" Woody asks.

"The school board meets next week," Nelson says as he starts to twirl the baton around his head again. "Keep your fingers crossed."

Woody sees the streetlight at the corner go on. "You know what time it is?" he asks.

"If you're here, it must be dinnertime."

"How come you're not inside eating?"

"They're fighting."

"About what?"

Nelson shakes his head. "Nosy little thing, aren't you, Woody?"

"I like to keep up," he admits.

"Maybe you should find someone else to mooch off of tonight. I hear Mrs. Maurer is making chili con carne."

Woody shakes his head. "She makes it too hot. How long are your folks going to be fighting tonight?"

"Depends what's on TV," Nelson tells him.

Woody turns toward the house. The window is open. He can hear Mrs. Grillo shouting at Mr. Grillo. There's a long silence. Woody guesses that means it's Mr. Grillo's turn. When Mrs. Grillo catches her breath, she goes at him all over again. Woody gets a whiff of something that smells a lot like pot roast. It's one of his favorites. The longer it cooks, the better it tastes, too. He sits down on the back steps. For Mrs. Grillo's pot roast, he can wait awhile.

"My folks never fight," he says. "Never even raise their voices."

"Your dad's in prison, Woody," Nelson reminds him. "During visiting hours with all the other people around, who would? It'd be too embarrassing."

Woody shrugs. "I wouldn't know about that," he tells him. "I never went up there."

Nelson tosses his baton in the air again. "Not once?" he asks. "It's two years since your father went up."

"I got better things to do on Saturdays than spend six hours on a Trailways bus."

"Just because you do a bad thing doesn't mean you're a bad person."

Woody shakes his head. "Where did you dig that one up?" he asks. "Montel?"

"Oprah," Nelson admits. "I been saving it for you, Woody."

"Well, you can keep it. I don't want it."

"Hey, your dad's not the first person who ever got in trouble with the law," Nelson says.

"He was a cop," Woody reminds him. "He was supposed to be the law."

"Your mom sees him, doesn't she?"

"She doesn't have any choice." Woody sighs. "She's married to him."

"So you're being a jerk," he says, throwing the baton in the air.

"So why don't you mind your own business, Nelson?"

"My friends are my business," Nelson says as he goes back to tossing the baton into the air.

Woody shrugs. If Nelson thinks they're friends, he's not going to correct him. He can't help hoping Nelson doesn't go around telling people that they're friends, though. He'd never hear the end of it.

Woody hears Mrs. Grillo inside. If anything, she's got her second wind. Nelson has caught his baton probably fifty times now, and Woody can see he's getting worn out. When Nelson collapses next to him on the back steps, Woody can hear him panting. The skin on his shoulder is moist.

Woody takes a sniff. He can't smell Nelson's skin, though. He wonders if maybe Nelson doesn't get B.O. like regular boys. He wouldn't be surprised. Wouldn't Nelson be surprised if Woody leaned over and kissed his shoulder? Not that he's attracted to Nelson. Nelson's a boy, after all. But he's so much like a girl, Woody can't help being curious.

"Your doctor says it's okay to practice so hard?" Woody asks.

"You think I should tell him?" Nelson asks.

"You got a lot of guts," Woody says. "That's all I can say." He gets up. "Maybe I better get going."

"It's not going to be all that long," Nelson assures him. "I think they're over the worst of it."

"Not tonight."

As he walks back to the street, he can feel Nelson's eyes on him. He hears Nelson coughing. Woody turns around. Nelson's disappeared. So maybe he wasn't looking at him after all.

He sees a light on at the Bruegmanns'. They're usually good for one of those chicken potpies. They're from the store, but Woody likes them a lot. Or he could go back to the Hirsts' for the cobbler. He decides to head home instead. Besides, he's not hungry anymore.

II

The next morning, Woody sees the macaroni-and-cheese pan in the fridge. It's on the top shelf between the milk and eight bottles of salad dressing. Carefully, he removes the aluminum foil on top. If anything, it looks even more disgusting than it did last night.

He takes the milk out of the fridge, puts the carton on the counter. The cornflakes are in the cupboard. He grabs a bowl and starts to fill it with the milk. When the milk is two-thirds up to the top of the bowl, he starts to sprinkle the cornflakes into the milk.

"Why do you do it that way?" Joel asks. "It's so weird."

"It tastes the same," Woody says, sticking two pieces of white bread in the toaster.

Joel's only nineteen, but already he's developing a pot. He's got a wide face, and there's a rubber band at the back of his head for the last three inches of his stringy black hair to go through. Until two months ago Joel lived at home. But he got married, and now he and Cheryl Ann live with her folks. Usually, he comes to the house for breakfast on his way to community college.

Although he doesn't ever tell Joel, Woody's glad for the company. Their mom doesn't have to be at school till ten o'clock, so usually she sleeps in.

"Cheryl Ann's going to have a baby," Joel says while he's buttering the toast.

"Is that a good thing?" Woody asks.

"Cheryl Ann's happy about it," Joel tells him. "I'm going to have to quit school."

"Mom's going to be upset about that."

"That's why I'm telling you and I'm not telling her," Joel

says. "Not yet, anyway. They're taking guys on over at the boat repair."

"You could get a job there?"

"Why not?"

"After what Dad did to them?" Woody exclaims.

"I don't see why that makes such a big difference," Joel says.

"He went to jail for it," Woody protests.

Joel shrugs. "Well, it's about the only place hiring."

As Joel rinses his coffee mug in the sink, Woody spots their mother's checkbook on the table by the door.

"Don't forget you got to balance the checkbook," he tells Joel.

Joel smiles. "That's your job now, Woody. Get used to it."

"Why can't she do it herself?" Woody groans.

"Your guess is as good as mine," Joel says as he steps outside and closes the door behind him.

Woody picks up the checkbook. He recognizes Joel's numbers the last time he did the balance. He does a guesstimate in his head of what his mom has written checks for since then and the three deposits she's made. The result is four dollars more than what his allowance is.

III

English is the only class that Woody and Nelson have together. But he sits in the second row, and Nelson sits in the back, so he's only half aware that Nelson's not there. There's a knock on the door. Before Mr. Czerny says anything, the door opens. It's Mrs. Wilser, the principal. She's got gray hair, and she kind of waddles like a big old bird. As she talks to Mr. Czerny, Woody can hear the classroom getting very quiet. Mr. Czerny is shaking his head.

Mrs. Wilser turns to the class, clears her throat. "There's bad news, boys and girls," Mrs. Wilser says. "It's Nelson. He had a bad asthma attack last night. By the time the ambulance came, it was too late."

The class is silent. Woody knows what "too late" means, but as long as Mrs. Wilser doesn't explain in words, it's still okay.

Mr. Czerny stands next to Mrs. Wilser. He's looking at her, waiting just like everyone else. But Mrs. Wilser's not talking. She dabs her eyes with a Kleenex and leaves the classroom.

"Nelson passed," Mr. Czerny tells the class.

"Passed?" one of the girls asks. "You mean Nelson died?"

Mr. Czerny nods. "Nelson's dead."

If Woody was home, it might be different. But he and Nelson weren't friends at school. He didn't get upset when his dad got arrested, did he? Not even when his mom was carrying on like the world was coming to an end. Why should he act upset here?

When the noon bell rings, the kids don't go into their usual stampede for the cafeteria. Some of the girls, cheerleaders mostly, are hugging each other and crying. Most of the boys straggle behind, not saying anything much. The lines in the lunchroom are very quiet. It's almost eerie.

Woody's mom is standing behind the steam counter, dishing out today's hot meal. It's spaghetti with a little sauce and a lot of cheese mixed in. When his mom hands a plate to him, he can see her lips moving a little, but he can't make out the words. Her eyes are wet. Whatever she was saying has to be about Nelson, he figures.

There's one table he always sits at. The other five boys who sit there are regulars, too. It's like an official club, and they don't need newcomers. After his dad went to prison, Woody wasn't sure if he should sit there anymore. But none of the boys ever said anything, so Woody figured it was okay to stay.

Billy Knause is already halfway through his spaghetti. Marty Kuhlman is twirling his spaghetti around on his fork. By the time he stops twirling, the spaghetti ball is too big to fit into his mouth. He gives it his best shot anyway, and as Woody sits down Marty is spitting his spaghetti back onto his plate.

Woody looks across the table at J. D. McEnroe. McEnroe brings his lunch. Usually, it's a sandwich with a lot of alfalfa sprouts popping out all over. Ralph Izbecki only gets desserts. Today he has two red Jell-Os and three pieces of apple pie on his tray.

The cheerleader types are sitting two tables away.

Woody can't help looking over at them now. It's where Nelson used to sit. He sees Marty looking over there, too. When Marty goes back to attacking his spaghetti, he has got this crazy smile on his face.

"What's so funny?" Woody asks.

"Nothing's funny," Marty assures him. But by now the crazy smile is more like a crazy grin.

"Tell, Marty!" McEnroe says. "What's so hilarious?"

"Two, four, six, eight," Marty says under his breath. "Nelson's going to suffocate."

"That's disgusting," J. D. McEnroe says.

"Don't take this personally," Billy Knause says, "but you are one sick dude, Marty."

Woody sees Billy and J. D. exchange glances. They're both shaking their heads, but they're smiling.

"Give me a *D*!" Billy whispers.

"Give me an *E*!" J. D. says.

"Give me an *A*!" Billy says.

Even before J. D. gets to the last letter, it's only a few seconds before all the other boys are laughing. Woody can't help it. By the time he joins in, everyone's out of control. As the kids at the other tables stare at the boys, it just gets worse. Tears are streaming down their faces, and they're pounding the table with their fists.

When the bell rings, the boys get up from the table. Woody starts down the corridor. He's got Mrs. Blackburn for algebra. He feels someone tugging at his sleeve. It's Marsha Krulis. She's one of the cheerleaders, and she's crying.

"What's wrong with you, Woody?" she asks. "How could you laugh like that?"

Woody shakes his head. "He just lived near me. That's all."

IV

It's almost dark. She brought home today's spaghetti, but it's not for supper. She's making something, for once. Chicken. She coats the pieces with Shake 'n' Bake and sticks them in the oven.

"What's wrong with the spaghetti?" Woody asks.

"I'm saving it," she says. "For your father."

"You think it's going to keep?" Woody asks. "Even in the fridge, four years is a long time."

"Don't get smart. You know what I mean. I'm taking it up to him Saturday," his mom tells him. "Besides, we need something special tonight. We should eat together, something nice, like a family."

"Why? What's special about tonight?"

"Nelson?" she says, like it's a question.

Woody shrugs. "It's okay."

"It's not okay," his mother says as she sets the forks and knives on the dining table. "Such a funny little kid. Maybe if he'd lived longer, he would have outgrown that cheerleader business."

"Why?" Woody asks. "What difference would it have made?"

"His life could have meant something," his mom explains.

Woody nods. When his mom goes back to the kitchen, he leaves the house. He knows where he's going, but he's not in any hurry to get there. Just as the streetlights go on, he sees the Grillos' house. There's cars parked all along the street, and the house is all lit up. Big family. They've got relatives coming from all over.

He sees something on the lawn. It's pink. As he walks over, he sees it's one of the tassels from Nelson's baton. When he hears a door slam, he looks up. It's Nelson's dad. He's got very black hair, and he's wearing a dark suit, too.

"Woody?" he asks. "Do you want to come in?"

Woody shakes his head. "I—I can't, Mr. Grillo," he stammers. "I'm sorry."

"I know you are, son," Mr. Grillo says. "Mrs. Grillo and I always appreciated how nice you were to Nelson. Not all the boys were."

"I got to go, Mr. Grillo," Woody says. "My mom's cooking. She'll get mad if I'm late."

Before Mr. Grillo can say anything more, Woody runs home. He's crying now, and he doesn't want Mr. Grillo to see.

V

Woody sits on the Trailways bus. His mother is next to him, looking out the window. There's an aluminum pan on his lap. It weighs a ton. He's playing with the foil on top. Inside is the spaghetti from school. He still can't believe his mother is taking a batch to his father.

"Dad actually likes this crap?" Woody asks.

His mother turns toward him. Her hair's done and she's got on a dress. Even if the food is crap, she always tries to look nice for her visits. "He says it's a lot tastier than what they serve in prison."

Woody starts to laugh. "Prison food is worse than this? You got to be kidding."

"That's what your father says."

"They should tell more people about that," Woody says. "They should put it on the news."

"What for?"

"It would lower the crime rate, Mom!"

"Oh, Woody! You're just making jokes on account of you're nervous about seeing your dad."

She pats his hand. She looks into his eyes. "It's nice of you, coming up to the prison like this," she says. "He's going to appreciate it, Woody."

Woody nods. But he's not doing it for his dad. He's not doing it for his mom, either. He's doing it because Nelson said he was a jerk if he didn't.

"Where did you get that?" his mom asks.

"Get what?"

She's pointing to the pink tassel Woody is toying with.

Woody shrugs.

"Don't you remember where you got it?"

For a moment, Woody feels the impulse to shove the thing back into the pocket of his jeans. But he's been toying with it all morning, and he doesn't feel like letting go of it yet.

"I got it from my friend," he tells his mom.

"That's nice, Woody," she says, but she doesn't ask which friend. It's funny, but it's okay.

She goes back to looking out the window.

He goes back to toying with the tassel.

Almost all my stories are set in small towns. The characters have lived there all their lives and will probably go on living there till the end of time. That's wishful thinking on my part. My parents were always on the move, and I don't want to remember how many schools I went to as a kid. I would have liked nothing more than to settle down, stay put. Lately, I've wondered if writing is my way of experiencing what I missed. Are my characters friends and neighbors I would have liked? Sometimes I think it must be so. Otherwise, I doubt I'd feel so at home with the characters in "Picky Eater."

When I write, I try to capture life and make some sense of it. As I wrote "Picky Eater," though, I found myself increasingly confused about the point of what's going on here. For me, thirteen was exhilarating, bewildering, scary, and wildly inconclusive. It seemed just plain wrong to give Woody an awareness of what it all meant when I spent that year growing more and more clueless. All I can say is, I wouldn't have missed it for the world, but once was enough. I sincerely doubt many people could survive it twice.

Stephen Roos

Stephen Roos was born in New York City, attended Loomis School in Windsor, Connecticut, and graduated from Yale. After working in publishing for twelve years, he turned to writing. His first novel for kids, *My Horrible Secret*, was published in 1983. His most recent novels are *The Gypsies Never Came* and *Recycling George*. He now lives in Litchfield County, Connecticut. At present he is collaborating with his partner, David Wolfe, on an adult novel set in the fashion industry.

Such Foolishness

Maureen Ryan Griffin

They say it's a difficult
stage. But what I remember
from that time
is the sultry summer day
rain came through the sun
to release me
from the childhood stretched
tight over my chafing skin.
I ran into the street,
the tom-tom beat of the rain
calling in a language
my feet had to answer,
my dog following at my heels
as though the scent of some beast
were leading her on. Steam snaked
from the pavement as the rain hissed.

My soles absorbed the heat, up
through the white cotton T-shirt
that clung to my new-found curves.
Finally I believed
the road would lead me out,
that I would shed that house
like the rim left behind
when I emerged from my bath
rosy, sacrificial. I swear
I saw my dog slink away
in disgust, snorting
at being taken in
by such foolishness—
but she was spayed as a puppy,
what did she know of it,
poor thing? I stayed
on the street, flung out
my arms, danced on.

There's a lot I remember about being thirteen: Having a big crush on Tommy Eliason and being crushed when, after having been a basketball cheerleader all season, he said to me, "You know, Maureen, if you want someone to like you, you ought to do *something, be a cheerleader or something." My mother telling me that girls could "get in trouble" slow dancing. Getting into trouble with Sister Pierre for reading books under my desk during math class. How utterly humiliating it was when Anthony Kupeniski pulled my chair out from under me just as I was sitting down, and I landed on the floor, my underwear showing (I went to a Catholic school and wore a gray-and-blue-plaid jumper—ugghhh!) How envious I was of all the "popular girls" who wore bikini underwear. How I felt seeing the stain in my underwear from my first period the morning after my eighth-grade graduation. (Was I the only thirteen-year-old preoccupied with underwear? This is the kind of question I always asked myself when I was thirteen. Was I the only one . . . ?) There's more—a lot more—I could tell you about the "difficult stage" of thirteen. But the energy and joy that coursed through my body, the anticipation of growing up and being on my own was so much a part of being thirteen, too! That dance in summer rain was a celebration of being alive inside my own skin, and as I inhaled the scent of wet asphalt—a smell I still love—I knew that it was a moment to keep.*

Maureen Ryan Griffin

Maureen Ryan Griffin is the author of a book of poems titled *When the Leaves Are in the Water*, and is also a radio commentator and a writing teacher. She lives in Charlotte, North Carolina, with her husband, daughter, son, cat, and dog, and she still dances in the rain from time to time.

Noodle Soup for Nincompoops

Ellen Wittlinger

Everybody else in seventh-grade honors English had groaned at the assignment, "I Am a Camera," but I thought it would be fun—three pages about anything your invisible "camera" noticed over the weekend. After spending most of Saturday at David Segal's bar mitzvah and Sunday afternoon at the mall with Liza and Harper, it didn't take me long to write "How to Flirt Without Showing Your Braces." Even Liza thought it was funny, and it was mostly about her. Actually, that's probably why she liked it; Liza is her own favorite subject these days.

I guess I notice things other kids don't. I like watching people. Most kids I know don't shut up long enough to notice anybody else; they're constantly yelling and wiggling around so *they* get noticed. David Segal's bar mitzvah party was so loud, I saw three grown-ups popping ibuprofen before they even served lunch. Liza, who's been my best friend since birth, or possibly earlier, is always right in the middle of the action. I'm usually standing on the edge of the crowd, hoping *not* to be noticed. It's always been that way, and neither of us has ever minded.

But now, according to Liza, I do way too much watching and not nearly enough flirting. Up until this year, neither of us talked to boys. We agreed they were aliens. But ever since Harper showed up, Liza is suddenly all about the opposite sex. "Who likes who" takes up three quarters of her conversation.

When Mr. Chrisman asked me to stay after class for a few minutes, I figured he wanted to talk to me about my essay. Mr. C is always complimenting me on my writing. Sure enough, he waved it in front of me and smiled. "Maggie, I knew you were a good writer," he said, "but I had no idea until now how funny you could be!" Even if I *did* have braces, I'd smile at Mr. Chrisman, who, in my opinion, is the best teacher at South Hadfield Middle School (and also really cute).

"You're such a natural writer—why is it you've never written anything for the *Newsflash*?" he asked me. Mr. C is the adviser for the school newspaper, the *Weekly Newsflash*, and he's always trying to recruit kids to write stuff for it. I guess it's hard to fill four pages every week with sports scores, lunch menus, and articles about how much toilet paper gets stolen from the girls' bathroom.

I shrugged. "I'm not that interested in writing *facts*. You know. I like to make things up."

He nodded. "Well, your essay gave me an idea. How would you like to write an advice column for the newspaper?"

I had to laugh. "What kind of advice could *I* give anybody? How to be invisible?"

Mr. C's smile disappeared. "Do you really think you're invisible?"

I shrugged. "To most kids. I don't care, though."

"I think of you as quiet but certainly not invisible. Anyway, for this job keeping a low profile is an asset." Mr. C motioned for me to sit down in the chair next to his desk. "Here's my idea. You wouldn't be writing a *real* advice column; it would be funny, something to get more kids interested in reading the paper. To begin with, I'd write a few letters with silly questions, and you could come up with funny answers. We'd tell kids that if they want to ask you questions, they can leave them in my box in the main office, and I can give them to you after class. That way, no one will know who you are."

"You mean, I wouldn't be answering the questions as Maggie Cluny? I'd make up a name? I'd be somebody else?"

"That's right. Make up a name. You can name the whole column whatever you want, just so it's funny. I think if we set it up as humorous from the beginning, kids will get the idea and write you funny questions."

The idea crept around in my mind. I could say whatever I wanted to as long as I wasn't Maggie Cluny. I'd have an alter ego, like Clark Kent and Superman. "But won't people find out it's me?"

"Well, that's the thing. In order to keep it secret, you couldn't tell *anybody.* Not even your best friends. I think the mystery aspect will add to the fun of it—everybody will be guessing who it is." Mr. Chrisman sat forward, his hands on his knees. "So, what do you think? Interested?"

"Yeah, I am. Can I think about it overnight?"

"Sure, sure. Meanwhile, I'll try my hand at a few letters, in anticipation!"

Why didn't anybody *my* age ever smile at me like Mr. C did? Sometimes I felt like I must already be thirty. I'd skipped right over the so-called "best years of my life" right into elderly boredom.

By the time I got to my locker, Liza was sitting on the floor, her head drooping over her books, her long blond-streaked hair hiding her face. She looked up when she heard me coming.

"Where have you *been*? Everybody left already. Robbie Piersall's mother picked him up, and he asked me if I needed a ride home, but you weren't here!"

"Sorry. I was talking to Mr. . . . Meadows . . . about the geography test."

"Ugh, geography." She got to her feet and dusted off the butt of her low-rise jeans, then readjusted her shirt so her belly button peeked out. You aren't allowed to have your stomach bare in school, but Liza always wears that stretchy material you can pull down or push up, depending on the occasion.

"Why did you want a ride?" I asked her, carefully changing the subject from my recent whereabouts. "It only takes us fifteen minutes to walk, and the weather's nice."

Liza sighed. "Maggie, God. I don't care about the *ride*. Robbie wanted me in his car! Don't you get it?"

"Oh." I hated it when Liza acted like I was the dumbest geek on earth. "Well, how was I supposed to know you liked Robbie Piersall? I thought you were crazy about David Segal—you were yesterday!" The turnover in Liza's boyfriends was hard to keep up with; she fell in love more often than most people brushed their teeth.

"I *am*. I don't think I even like Robbie, but maybe he likes *me*. Now I'll never know."

"I don't see how one car ride would have proved anything," I grumbled.

"That's because you just don't *get* stuff, Maggie. Honestly, sometimes you don't even seem like you're really thirteen!"

I guess she hadn't heard the news that I was actually thirty in disguise. "Well, sometimes you don't either," I said. "Sometimes you seem like you're about eighteen!"

Liza's pout turned up at the corners. "You really think so? Because of my hair?" She hooked her arm through mine and turned into my best friend again. "Wait till you hear what David said to me after math today. . . ."

"How's this?" I said, handing Mr. Chrisman a sheet of paper. I'd been working on the idea since I left school the day before, and I was proud of the final product.

"'Noodle Soup for Nincompoops; by Faustina Intelligentsia. No question too stupid to answer.'" He gave me his big, full-of-teeth smile. "You're going to do the column!"

"Do you like the name?" I asked.

"I love Faustina Intelligentsia—it's silly and pompous—perfect for a humor column. But I'm not sure I get 'Noodle Soup—'"

"I was trying to think of a name that would get people's attention, so I checked the paper to see what books were on the best-seller lists. There were all these books for 'dummies' and 'idiots,' and then there were a couple of Chicken Soup books, so I thought if I combined both of them . . ."

He threw his head back and laughed, his brown hair falling in his face. If only there were *boys* as cool as Mr. C. "'Noodle Soup for Nincompoops'! It's great. You're going to be good at this, Maggie. I can tell already." He handed me some papers. "Take a look at these and see if you can come up with funny answers. You don't have to do them all, just two or three. And remember, don't let anyone see what you're doing!"

If popularity at school had anything to do with how much teachers liked you, I'd have a posse. Unfortunately, it seemed to work the opposite way. Liza and Harper were both standing in the hallway when I came around the corner. As I said, Liza has been my friend forever, but Harper was a new addition. She was really Liza's friend more than mine, although I didn't hate her or anything.

She hung around with more of the popular kids than Liza and I did; it was because of her we got invited to David Segal's bar mitzvah. But sometimes I felt like Liza and Harper were the best friends and I was just a dark, silent shadow following them around.

At least Liza looked happy to see me today. "There you are. Harper's mom is going to drive us to the mall."

"How come? Wasn't Robbie Piersall's mother available?"

"Ha-ha. Let's go—she's waiting."

I hung back. "You're really going to the mall again? We were just there on Sunday."

Liza narrowed her eyes and stared at me as if she was trying to send me a coded message. "So? It's *fun*."

"Oh, yeah, if your idea of fun is watching boys pick out jeans at Abercrombie."

Harper was studying the white crescents of her cuticles, staying out of the debate.

Liza sighed. "Come on, Maggie. We'll go to the food court and get sweet-potato fries."

"Can we go to the bookstore?" I asked.

Harper looked up. "No! When you go into the bookstore, you want to stay forever, and we have to wait for you!"

"Oh, like I didn't wait half an hour for you two to try on fifty shades of nail polish!"

Liza gave me a tight smile. "Maybe we could meet you someplace if you want to go to the bookstore."

I shook my head. "That's okay. You guys go. I don't feel

like being inside this afternoon anyway. I might go home and rake leaves."

Harper rolled her eyes. "You're kidding. *Rake leaves*?"

"I like doing it. It's relaxing."

"So is going to the mall!" Liza said.

"Don't beg her," Harper said, heading for the stairs.

Liza looked disappointed. "Okay, go do your chores. Maybe you can come over tomorrow or something."

"Yeah, maybe," I said. Liza ran to catch up with Harper, which I hated to see. When had Harper become so very important?

Robbie Piersall set two boxes of the *Weekly Newsflash* on a table in the hallway outside the Little Theater, where kids usually picked up their copies. I tried to be nonchalant as I sauntered over and reached into a box. Several other kids were right behind me.

"This is a really good issue," Robbie announced. I had the feeling he was looking at me, so I didn't look up. Actually, I almost never look at Robbie; he's the kind of person who looks you right in the eyeballs, even if you hardly know him. It makes me so nervous, I can't think straight.

"You're the editor; you have to think it's good," some eighth grader said as he walked past without grabbing a copy.

"No, really. There's a new column on page three—it's really funny."

I took my skinny newspaper and stood back against the

wall, where I could see people's reactions without them noticing. Not that they ever noticed me anyway. This morning, though, my heart was beating so loud, I was afraid they'd look around to see where all the noise was coming from.

I opened the paper to page three, like everybody else. There it was:

Noodle Soup for Nincompoops
by Faustina Intelligentsia
"No question too stupid to answer!"

"Ha! Did you read this?" Jillie Randolph said. "Listen!" And she began to read my column out loud to the assembled group:

"Dear Faustina,
I am madly in love with my boyfriend, but my mother keeps calling it 'puppy love.' I hate that! How can I get her to stop?
—Teenager in Love

Dear Teenager in Love,
Poor you. Have you considered chewing up her bedroom slippers?
—Faustina Intelligentsia"

As Jillie was reading the column some kids had come up to look over her shoulder while others stood nearby, listening. They all laughed at my answer. Or rather, *Faustina's* answer.

"Who wrote that?" Adam Levine asked as he grabbed a paper out of the box.

"It doesn't say." Patrick Deveraux, an eighth grader, was sharing a paper with his girlfriend, Ellie Something-or-Other. "There's more." He read the second letter aloud:

> "Dear Faustina,
> I'm crazy about a girl who's two years older than me. I lied to her about my age, but now I'm afraid she'll find out and hate me for lying to her. What should I do?
> —Tangled Web
>
> Dear Tangled Web,
> Well, dearie, you have two choices: Keep lying until she tells everybody what a big phony you are, or find a girl two years younger and let her do the lying.
> —Faustina Intelligentsia"

The first bell rang, but nobody moved. Jillie started in again, reading the last letter:

> "Dear Faustina,
> I have a crush on my sister's boyfriend, and I think he likes me, too. Is it okay for me to go for it?
> —Better-Looking Sister

Dear Better-Looking Sister,
Sure, sweetheart, go right ahead. Of course, it's also okay for your sister to kick your butt from here to Tuscaloosa. Duh.
—Faustina Intelligentsia"

"These are funny!" Ellie said. "Somebody must know who wrote them."

"Here's a clue," Patrick said. "It says, 'If you have questions for Faustina Intelligentsia, please leave them in Mr. Chrisman's mailbox in the main office.' So it must be somebody who's on the staff."

"Who wrote this, Robbie?" Melanie Cross said. "You must know."

Robbie shrugged. "It's a secret."

"Oh, come on," Ben Anders said. "You're the editor."

"I don't know. Really. Mr. Chrisman is the only one who knows."

Everybody was talking about my column and trying to guess who'd written it. They were guessing all the obviously funny kids—the guys who can break up the teachers, the girls whose sarcasm can drop an enemy at fifty feet. When the second bell rang, I folded up my newspaper and walked off down the hall, invisible as ever. It was wonderful, but it was frightening, too. All these kids wanted to know who I was! Now I *really* didn't want them to find out because I knew they'd be disappointed that it was just me, Maggie Cluny.

It was almost impossible for Mr. Chrisman to get our class to settle down.

"Come on, Mr. C. Who is it?"

"Why does it have to be a secret, anyway?"

"We won't tell anybody!"

He smiled and shook his head. "Give it up," he said. "I am an excellent keeper of secrets."

I turned into a piece of petrified wood, afraid to move so much as a finger lest I call attention to myself. I didn't dare even glance at Mr. Chrisman.

"I would think whoever is writing the column would *want* people to know who he is. He's good!"

"It's not necessarily a *he*, Robbie," Liza said. "It could be any of us."

"Yes, it could. Isn't a little mystery fun?" Mr. C said. "And now on to the mystery of your vocabulary tests."

After school I saw little knots of kids huddled over the *Newsflash*, laughing. Amazingly, I was a hit.

"Who do you think it is?" Liza asked me while we were walking home.

Mr. C had told me not to tell even my best friends, but I wouldn't have told Liza anyway. Her record for secret keeping is about twelve seconds.

"Who do you think?" I asked her back, hoping not to have to tell another out-and-out lie.

"At first I thought Robbie had probably written it himself—he was making such a big deal out of it—but now I don't think so." She gave me a sideways glance.

"No?" I picked a yellowing leaf from a tree and studied it carefully.

"No. Who do you think it is?"

"How should I know?" I said.

"Is it *you*?" Liza said, suddenly turning in front of me so I had to stop walking.

I was so surprised, I jumped. "*Me*? You really think I could write something like that?" I could feel my pupils jumping around in my eyes.

"You can be funny sometimes. Around me. Besides, you're all buddy-buddy with Mr. Chrisman."

I didn't say anything. I just stared at Liza like she was a skunk in my path while I tried to decide how on earth to convince her I was not Faustina Intelligentsia. It turned out silence was the right move.

"Oh, don't look so shocked!" she said. "I guess it couldn't really be you, could it? I mean, you wouldn't do anything as outrageous as that, would you?"

My silence began to heat up as we continued walking.

"I mean, I wish you *were* Faustina Intelligentsia. That would be so cool."

"And I'm not cool enough as I am? Is that what you mean?"

"Don't get mad about it. You're just not the kind of person who's funny in public." She gave my arm a little punch. "It's okay. *I* know you're funny."

I wished I could tell her the truth, that everybody at school was laughing at *my* writing. But I couldn't, and it didn't seem fair that she was ragging on me again, so I said, "At least we know it isn't Harper who's writing it. I've never heard her say anything the least *bit* funny."

We stopped to pet Mrs. Grayson's collie so we wouldn't have to talk anymore.

Mr. Chrisman was ecstatic about the reaction kids were having to my column. During the next few weeks, we got two dozen letters in the box. Most kids understood that the column was supposed to be a spoof, and they wrote silly questions about things like whether or not to cut their hair and whether you should kiss on the first date. Questions Faustina could have fun with.

While I was playing with Faustina, Liza began to spend more time with Harper. Sometimes they invited me along, and sometimes they didn't, which was fine. Shopping is boring. Besides, I never really felt comfortable with Harper, anyway. I missed Liza, though—I missed her a lot.

Meanwhile, the kids were still trying to figure out who Faustina was. For a while they were evenly divided between those who thought Robbie Piersall was writing the column and those who thought it might be Pam Ackerman, a girl with a big attitude who'd transferred to our school this year from a school in New York City. The idea was that anybody who'd lived in New York was automatically funny, although I'd personally never seen her crack a smile. Except for Liza, nobody suspected me, not for a moment. I pretended to Mr. C that this was great, but secretly, I was getting a little depressed about it. Nobody had a clue that Faustina Intelligentsia could live inside somebody like me.

Now I was always the last person to leave English class. Mr. C would put the letters on a corner of his desk so I could whisk them up without attracting too much attention, even if he was talking with somebody. One afternoon there was a single letter lying there. I scooped it up and dumped it in my backpack to read when I got home. Liza and Harper had plans after school with another girl, Annie, whom I didn't know very well, so I walked home alone. It was starting to get cold out now, which made me remember walking home with Liza on wintry days, how we'd put our hoods up over our ears and run until we got warmed up, then dawdle the rest of the way, as usual.

By the time I got home, I'd forgotten about the letter. I did my Spanish and geography homework, then went downstairs to help Mom make potato latkes for dinner. It wasn't until nine o'clock that I remembered Faustina's letter. I dug it out of my backpack, opened the envelope, and got ready to laugh.

The question was neatly typed with no errors and run out on a sheet of canary yellow paper. I shivered the minute I saw it.

> Dear Faustina,
> I'm having a problem with my best friend. I've made some new friends lately, and I don't think

she likes them. I feel like I'm stuck in the middle between my old friend, who's sort of quiet, and the new ones, who like to party. What should I do?
—Stuck

There was no doubt in my mind—it was from Liza. For one thing, she was a very good typist, and I happened to know that her mother kept a big stack of yellow computer paper in her desk drawer. Liza certainly had new friends, who liked to party. And one old dull one. Suddenly, I felt sick to my stomach and lay down on my bed. Liza was having a "problem" with me. She wanted to hang out with her new friends and I was holding her back. God, it never occurred to me that Liza wanted to dump me, but I could see she was asking Faustina Intelligentsia for permission to do just that.

And then I wondered if Liza had figured out who Faustina Intelligentsia really was. If so, she'd know that *I'd* know she sent the letter. We'd used that yellow paper ourselves lots of times. Maybe she was warning me: Either go along with my new friends, or get out of the way.

My best friend since forever was getting ready to throw me overboard, and I was supposed to write something funny about it and *publish it in the school newspaper*! It was impossible—I couldn't do it. I couldn't even think about it! Except I couldn't *stop* thinking about it either.

After an hour of dithering, I decided I wasn't going to get anything else done anyway, so I crawled into bed and turned out the light, even though I knew it was going to be impossible to go to sleep. In the dark I started wondering what Faustina Intelligentsia would say to Liza.

It was funny. I had a picture in my mind of who Faustina was, and she was nothing like me. She had wild red hair piled up on her head like a messy bird's nest, with pencils and feathers and beads all wound around in it. She was about twenty-five years old and wore granny boots and thrift-store clothes and black lipstick. And her laugh was loud enough to make everybody look at her, even in the middle of someplace as noisy as David Segal's bar mitzvah party. She was very cool and definitely *not* invisible.

Every time I sat down to think of an answer to a question, I imagined her putting her boots up on the table and cackling over the smart-aleck answer. It wasn't that I wanted to *be* like her, but I really liked having her inside my head, letting me see things the way she saw them. I wondered what Mr. C would think of her. He'd probably like Faustina more than me, since she was funny *and* a grown-up. He probably liked red hair.

When I finally fell asleep, I dreamed I lived in the custodian's closet at school. Mr. Chrisman was the only person who knew I was there, and he brought me bowls of noodle soup for every meal. I didn't mind it at all. When I woke up in the morning, I knew what Faustina Intelligentsia would say to Liza.

> Dear Stuck,
> What you should do, dearie, is *get out of the middle*! Two roads diverged, and all that. You

can't go both ways, unless you're a real split
personality. Here's the question: Do you want to
end up eating noodle soup with the nincompoop,
or do you want to have a good time? Do you
really have to ask?

—Faustina Intelligentsia

It was the right answer. Faustina was always right.

The rest of that week Liza acted the same as she always did, nice to me one minute, then running off with Harper the next. Until Friday, the day the *Weekly Newsflash* came out.

Once again everybody was giggling about the column. They couldn't believe they still didn't know who wrote it. I caught up with Liza as she headed into Mr. C's room for English.

"Got your *Newsflash*, I see." I wondered if she'd read her answer yet, if she'd take Faustina's advice.

Liza turned and glared at me. "Yes, I do."

Her look scalded my cheeks. "So, after school do you want to—"

"I'm busy after school," she said, flinging her half-and-half hair in my face as she turned away from me. "I'm going to Harper's. She's having a party tonight."

"Oh, okay." But she wasn't hanging around to hear my response. She'd already *had* a response, from Faustina Intelligentsia, and she was obviously following the advice to the letter.

I couldn't concentrate very well in English; I kept

sneaking looks at Liza, who had taken the seat farthest away from mine, even though it meant sitting in the front row. Could this really be happening? Would Liza really stop being my friend after all these years because of some silly newspaper column? But no, I reminded myself, she'd wanted to get rid of me before that. The column just gave her permission.

I let Liza fly out of class before I gathered up my books and trudged to the door. Mr. C gave me a big smile, and I gave him a halfhearted one in return. Then, just as I got to the door, Robbie Piersall came up behind me and bent his head close to my ear.

"It's you, isn't it?" he whispered. "I know it is."

"What?" I was shocked to see his grinning mouth and blue eyes so close to mine.

He pulled me off to the side of the hall, so we were out of the traffic flow. "You're Faustina, aren't you? I know it." When I still struggled to speak, he added, "Don't worry. I'm not going to tell anybody. The column is great—it's the best thing in the *Newsflash*!"

I dared to glance into his eyes as they bored into mine. Finally, I found my voice. "Thanks. How did you—"

"Two reasons. First of all, most of the bigmouths around here would have already told people if they were writing it. You aren't like that. And secondly, I saw your 'I Am a Camera' essay. Mr. C left a stack of papers lying around the newspaper office, and yours was on top, so I read it. I didn't put two and two together right away, but suddenly, it hit me. If there was anybody else who could write that well, I'd know about them."

My mouth fell open. "I didn't think anybody would figure it out. I mean, I'm sort of invisible around here."

"You just think you are. I've noticed you before."

Then we both turned red and looked at the floor.

I wanted to run away, but the only excuse I could think of, that I had to meet Liza to walk home, was a lie. Finally, I just said. "I should get going."

Robbie nodded. "If you ever need a ride home or anything . . . I mean, my mom drives me and . . . you don't live that far away."

He knew where I *lived*?

"I told Liza a few weeks ago we'd give you guys a ride, but I guess she didn't tell you."

She *told* me, she just made it sound more like *her* invitation than mine.

"Actually, if your mom doesn't mind . . . I would kind of like a ride."

"Great!" Robbie smiled as we walked to the seventh-grade lockers. We walked together, like it was a normal thing to do.

I didn't hear from Liza on Friday night, but who cared? Let her go to some dumb party with Harper. Robbie called and we talked on the phone for a while. Actually, we ran out of stuff to say to each other after about five minutes, so then we just sort of *breathed* together and laughed for another five.

On Saturday, Mom offered to take me to the mall for

new shoes, but I was afraid I'd run into the new best friends there, so I said I didn't feel like it. I sat at my desk doing homework and writing next week's "Noodle Soup for Nincompoops."

Robbie called Saturday night and wanted to know if I could go out with him, like to the movies. I couldn't believe this was happening to me! I got so nervous—what would we talk about for a whole evening?—that I told him my mother wouldn't let me go out alone with boys yet. I don't even know if that's true; I never had to ask her about it before. He said that was okay, that maybe next weekend we could get a group of kids to go!

As soon as I hung up the phone, I missed Liza terribly. It looked like I might just have my first boyfriend ever, and I didn't even have a best friend to talk to about it! Liza would know what to say if somebody asked her to the movies. I needed her! Twice I dialed her phone number, all but the last digit, then hung up. If she didn't want to be my friend, I wasn't going to beg her.

I slept late Sunday—Robbie had to work on a project for his science class, so I knew he wouldn't call until the evening. There wasn't much to do until then except read the Sunday papers and avoid my mother's questions about who that boy was who "keeps calling."

Just after noon the doorbell rang. Mom and Dad were in the backyard mulching the roses for winter, so I hauled myself off the couch and opened the door. There stood Liza, her lips pursed, her eyes blazing.

"I can't believe you, Maggie!" She started right in

yelling. "Doesn't our friendship mean *anything* to you? After all these years? You just tell me to 'get out of the middle' and go to parties with my new friends. You just wipe me out of your life like . . . like you're erasing a chalkboard!" The anger melted off her face, and before I knew it, she was standing there with her hands over her eyes, crying.

I pulled her inside the house, and she sniffed and rubbed her face on her sleeve, trying to get the mad back.

"Did you know it was me all along?"

"Of course I knew. Well, not immediately, but I kept thinking about it. Who else can write that funny? And I know you and Mr. Chrisman are crazy about each other, so of course he got you to do it. You thought your best friend wouldn't figure it out?"

"If you're my best friend, why did you write that letter to me?"

"I don't know. You've been so weird since we started hanging around with Harper. . . ."

"You're the one who started hanging around with Harper."

She shrugged. "Whatever. I wrote the letter to tell you . . . it's hard for me that you don't like my new friends that much. And I thought it would be a funny way to do it in a letter to your column. I knew you'd know it was me because of the yellow paper and all, but I didn't think you'd say, 'Fine, just go off with your new friends'!"

"But I thought you were saying I had to go along with

all your new friends or . . . get out of your way. I thought you were dumping me."

"You dumped me! You said, 'two roads diverge' and all that stuff." Her tears had finally dried up.

"I thought that was what Faustina Intelligentsia would tell you. You should get rid of your boring friend and hang out with the ones who want to party. It's not what *I* wanted you to do."

Liza stared at me, her mouth hanging slightly open. Then she took her fist and punched me on the arm. "You're nuts, Maggie. You're a crazy person. You told me to go hang out with other people even though you still want to be my best friend?"

"Of course I do. Who else would I hang out with?"

She hit me again, and then we hugged each other, briefly. Liza isn't really the huggy type. "If you ever do anything this dumb again, Maggie Cluny, you can be best friends with Faustina Intelligentsia or the nincompoop or whoever you are at the moment."

"I won't," I promised as we sank down onto the sofa. "So I guess this means you're stuck in the middle again."

She sighed. "The middle isn't so bad. At least I won't have to spend another entire weekend with Harper. Here I was all upset, and all she wanted to talk about was whether or not she should get her hair cut. I guess your weekend wasn't so hot either, huh?"

I smiled. "Liza, you won't even believe it."

At thirteen I thought nothing was cooler than spaghetti-strapped dresses. The one I'm wearing in the photograph was purchased for some party that seemed very important at the time but that I've now entirely forgotten. What I remember most about being thirteen is that it was a year full of fluctuation. One minute I felt so grown up, wearing high heels and bare-shouldered dresses to a boy-girl party, and the next I wanted to pull on my sweatshirt and tennis shoes and sit in my bedroom alone, dusting my horse statues.

At thirteen it was very difficult to feel comfortable. Some of my friends looked suddenly mature; others tried to act that way. Thirteen was the year my dog died and my best friend was unsympathetic. It was the year I realized that the kids from my neighborhood, the poorer kids, were almost never "popular." It was the year I found Eugene O'Neill and Tennessee Williams in the library and fell in love with playwriting. It was also the year I was so in love with the boy across the street that when he laid an arm lightly around my shoulders, I had to get up and walk away. Thirteen I remember as a year of many tears and much hope.

Ellen Wittlinger

Ellen Wittlinger was born in southern Illinois and has lived in Iowa, Oregon, and, for the past thirty years, Massachusetts. At the beginning of her writing career she wrote poetry, plays, and fiction for adults; during a stint as a children's librarian she began to write novels for teenagers.

Many of her books have been named ALA Best Books and Quick Picks; they've been nominated for a number of state reader's choice awards and have been named Junior Library Guild Selections. Her book *Hard Love* won a Lambda Literary Award and a Michael Printz Honor Award in 2000. Among her other books are *Lombardo's Law, What's in a Name, Gracie's Girl, Razzle, The Long Night of Leo and Bree,* and *ZigZag*. She is currently at work on her ninth novel for teens.

Squid Girl

Todd Strasser

Here's the bad news: A compost toilet doesn't flush. Here's the good news . . . Sorry, there is no good news. Compost toilets are severely beyond gross. Why are you being forced to think about compost toilets? Because it's spring vacation and your tree-hugging organic-fruit-and-nut-case parents have dragged you across several boring time zones via two airplanes, one smelly boat, and a tooth-loosening Jeep ride so that the three of you can spend a week squeezed into a mosquito-filled tent on this warm, moist, lush, green, tropical bug-infested island. According to the tree huggers, you are here to hike and snorkel and get back in touch with nature.

Here's what nature offers: Bugs. Bats. Crabs. And the compost toilet.

Here's what nature does not offer: Shopping. Mall. TV. Computer. Telephone.

In other words, you have been denied the minimum basic necessities for human survival.

Only one thing will keep you from going totally psycho: the beach.

At least you will go home tan.

It would be too much to ask for boys.

Wait!

There's a boy!

Under the hot orange sun, sitting on a towel on the flour-soft sand, you found him with Mom's super bird-watcher binoculars. He, and what appear to be his parents, are way down at the other end of this thin, crescent-shaped white beach. He is tall, dark, and may or may not be cute. Even with the binoculars, he is too far away to really tell.

But now you have hope.

And a plan.

Step one: When you return to this beach tomorrow, you will not be wearing the perfectly stupid clunky hiking boots your father insisted you wear today. You needed them to clomp down a rocky trail past big green fan palms and huge agave plants that look like giant green octopuses with pointy-spiky tentacles. Dad, aka Mr. Nature Man, said the local people call them century plants because they bloom once every sixty or eighty years and then shrivel up and die. Except after a hurricane, when they all bloom at once. This makes you wonder how these plants know when it's a hurricane, as opposed to a really nasty storm. Like, do they all watch the Weather Channel or something?

As if that weren't bad enough, Mr. Nature Man had to stop along the trail to show you the Wonderbra of spider-webs, made by the singularly disgusting brown-and-yellow golden orb spider. Mr. Nature Man insisted you touch the web and feel how strong it was. With great reluctance, you did, and you pray you will never be asked to again.

Anyway, tomorrow you will bring your new black Reef flip-flops.

Step two of your plan: Burn, baby, burn. Today, being the first day of vacation, you are ridiculously pale and in no way presentable to tall, dark boys who may or may not be cute. So as soon as Mom and Dad go off snorkeling in the glistening mouthwash-turquoise water, you towel off all the sunblock Mom insisted you slather on yourself. And then you get prone for the roast.

By evening you have a lobster-red sunburn. It hurts—but hey, no pain, no gain. Of course you've heard the warnings about skin cancer, and you promise yourself this is the last tan you'll get, at least until summer. In the tent you can hardly see how red you are because the only mirror is the size of a paperback book. Even if the mirror were larger, it would be hard to see because the "lights" in the tent run on solar power. Only, if they were any dimmer, you'd have to call them "darks." When you ask Mr. Nature Man how you can have solar power at night, he tells you about solar cells that store the energy during the day so you will have it after the sun goes down. This is what tree huggers love: toilets that never flush and lights that barely light. Go figure.

You play Scrabble with the pair-o-rents. Just before bedtime Mr. Nature Man takes you outside to look at the stars. You go mostly on the extremely slim chance that Travis might also be outside looking at the stars (you don't know what his name is, but you like the name Travis). You also go because the last time you and Mr. Nature Man went star-watching, you actually got to see a flaming orange fireball streak across the black sky, and it was awesome cool.

Outside the sky is so dark that the stars really do shimmer and sparkle. When you ask what all the little high-pitched eepy sounds are, Mr. Nature Man says, "Oh, just bats."

This leads to a brief lesson on why bats are our friends (they eat mosquitoes). Then you go back to the tent, where, thanks to your sunburn, you feel like a fireball yourself. But the good news is that you are genetically predisposed to tan, and by tomorrow you expect to have taken serious strides toward a deep, rich chocolate hue.

Major disappointment. Back at the beach the next day you have determined that Travis is truant. Perhaps it's just as well. This will give you another day to work on your appearance (such hard work, lying in the sun). Besides, the bats aren't such good friends after all. You woke up this morning covered with itchy, blotchy red mosquito bites.

So you resign yourself to one more day of sunning to increase the tan and decrease the blotches. Meanwhile, the tree huggers go off down the talcum-powder beach to search for shells, so at least you'll have some peace. But sun worship is interrupted by excited shouts of people in the water. Someone snorkeling has discovered a sea turtle. Not that you really care, but you are hot from the roast and it is definitely time to get wet.

You pull on your mask, snorkel, and flippers and dive in. The water is so clear, it feels like swimming in a giant aquarium. Almost by accident, you swim out to where the turtle is. By now two or three other snorkelers are splashing around with their flippers. Twelve feet below, sparse turtle grass grows on the sandy bottom like green hair on some old balding man's head. Two brown sea turtles flap lazily along, pausing here and there to graze in this underwater meadow.

And that's when some idiot swims right into you, banging his head into yours.

You both surface and pull off your masks. And . . . ohmigod!

"Travis?" you gasp.

"What?" he asks.

"Oh, nothing." But it's him! And he's really cute, even with those deep red lines where the mask pressed against his forehead and cheekbones and the yucky clear stuff that always drips out of people's noses when they snorkel.

"Cool turtles," he says.

"Yeah," you reply.

"You think it's a mom and her kid?" he asks.

"You mean because one's big and the other's smaller?"

"Well, sure."

"Turtles don't do that mommy-baby stuff," you explain, having learned this from Mr. Nature Man on some other trip. "But they're still really cute."

Travis treads water for a moment more. "Well, see ya." He pulls his mask and snorkel back on and swims away.

You tread water a little longer, watching the wake his flippers and snorkel leave behind. Why did you have to tell him he was wrong about mommy and baby turtles? Haven't you learned *anything* about boys? They hate being told they're wrong. Always.

Back on the beach, the tree huggers have returned with a treasure trove of pink-and-white cowrie shells, a few baby conks, and one slightly odoriferous sun-dried sea horse, which is a truly amazing find. Then comes the bad news: Mr. Nature Man announces that you've gotten too much sun. Two days at the beach is enough, so tomorrow you will hike to the ruins of the old sugar plantation.

This calls for extreme emergency action. Despite your mosquito blotches and recent sea-turtle blunder, you must find a way to walk down the beach and "bump into" Travis. It is imperative that you establish an uplink before you are dragged off into a different orbit. But going for a walk alone is totally out of the question. And you can't ask Mr. Nature Man because gorgeous Travis might find father types intimidating. So that leaves the Bird Woman.

"Want to go for a walk down the beach, Mom?" you

ask, hoping that she'll jump at the chance to bond with her thirteen-year-old daughter.

"Sure!" Mom's ready faster than you can say *instant message*. Together you head down the thin, crescent-shaped beach.

The walk turns out to be a real bonanza for the Bird Woman. She points out a brown-and-white osprey carrying a fish in its claws in the sky above and, circling even higher, a large black bird with a forked tail called a Magnificent Frigate. You don't tell her that you've got your eye on a different kind of magnificent wildlife. And lucky you, there he is about fifty feet away, knee-deep in the mouthwash, tossing a neon orange Frisbee to a smaller version of himself. A mini-Travis, as it were.

And just then, in what has to be one of the most remarkable strokes of luck ever, Mini-Travis launches the Frisbee high over his brother's head, and it lands, amazingly, on the soft white sand at your feet. Naturally, you bend down to pick it up. Travis turns and gestures with a little wave. You could send the Frisbee back to him with a mere flick of the wrist, but now Mini-Travis waves for the Frisbee as well. He is about 150 feet away, also knee-deep in the water, and a much more tempting target. You bring your arm back and whip the Frisbee in a high graceful arc, which ends precisely in Mini-Travis's hands.

"Great throw!" cheers the Bird Woman.

"Not bad," Travis agrees. He smiles for a moment, then turns around just in time to make a diving, splashing catch off Mini-Travis's next throw. When he stands up again, water drips from his soaked and glistening brown hair and runs down his slim bronzed body. He sends the Frisbee back to Mini-Travis without looking at you. And you sense, in a typhoon of disappointment, that he has already forgotten.

You continue down the beach, the Bird Woman chirping about the purple-throated hummingbird she saw at the feeder that morning and pointing out the little group of brown-and-white sandpipers scurrying on yellow stilt legs as they peck at the water's edge. You anxiously wonder if you once again blew it with that perfect throw to Mini-Travis. Did Travis think you were showing off? (You know you were.)

You and the Bird Woman reach the end of the beach and turn around. Now, instead of looking forward to seeing Travis, you dread it. He must think you're a show-off and a know-it-all. How did it all go so horribly wrong? How did you manage to ruin this vacation so fast? What are the chances the tree huggers will let you take a plane home this afternoon?

"Hey," someone says. It's Travis, standing in the water, his dark hair stringy and flecked with white sand. "My idiot brother has this problem. Maybe you can help."

Mini-Travis slogs through the shallows and points at Travis. "*He's* the idiot."

"Remember when we were snorkeling before and saw those turtles?" Travis asks. "When I was swimming back, I saw these three squids. Just hanging there in the water. Big eyes and tentacles and everything."

"Only they're cuttlefish," goes Mini-Travis.

"They're not fish, they're squids," Travis insists, and then turns to you with a look that says, *You tell him.*

"Well, uh, you're both right, in a way," you go.

Travis screws up his face. "How's that?"

"They're called 'cuttlefish,' but actually, they're in the cephalopod family, which includes squids and octopuses." It is extremely bizarre that you should possess this obscure and useless piece of knowledge. But after years of living with the Bird Woman and Mr. Nature Man, it is as natural to you as the names of baseball players are to boys.

"Don't forget the chambered nautilus," adds the Bird Woman.

"So you see," Mini-Travis gloats, "they *are* cuttlefish."

"But they're squids, too," goes Travis.

"No, they're in the same *family*, but they're *not* squids," goes Mini-Travis. "Just like octopuses aren't squids. Just like you were born without a brain." A second later he and his brother are engaged in a mammoth splashing war and have once again forgotten that you exist.

Feeling wretched and ignored, you continue down the beach with the Bird Woman. "Do you think I should have explained to them that the plural of *squid* in this case is *squid*, not *squids*?" she asks.

Having just made Travis look bad in front of his little brother, you shrug miserably. He must totally hate you now. You're a freak. A major nerd. Utterly unfit for social interaction with boys. The plural of "you blew it" in this case is "you blew it big-time."

And so, the next day, in a gloom of dejection, you and your new dark, rich tan accompany the tree huggers on the hike to the old sugar plantation ruins. After tromping for an hour through the humid green overgrowth, you stand in a sunny clearing and stare at a mound of old bricks while a park ranger lady wearing a tan uniform and a wide-brimmed khaki hat talks about the volcanic origins of this island. And how the Danes came in the 1600s and clear-cut the whole place to grow sugarcane. And how they imported mongooses to get rid of the rats, only the rats on this island live in trees while mongooses are not into tree climbing, so they ate all the snakes and lizards instead.

And that sounds exactly like the stupid, wrongheaded blunder you made by acting smart and making Travis look bad. You had a chance for happiness this vacation, and you lost it. You are a Frisbee-throwing possessor of useless knowledge. A geek. You do not deserve a boy. Your parents may be nature freaks, but you're a freak of nature. It's hopeless. You are . . . a loser.

"Hey, it's Squid Girl!" someone says.

You look up. Another group has just entered the clearing, and, incredibly, within this group are Travis and Mini-Travis and their parental unit. And Mini-Travis is pulling Travis toward you.

"My idiot brother says most shooting stars are only the size of a grain of sand," goes Mini-Travis. "Would you please tell him he's nuts."

"We learned about it in school," Travis counters.

"You're wacko," Mini-Travis demands. "They're stars."

"No, he's right," you answer. "Most of them are the size of a grain of sand or even a speck of dust. When they get to be the size of marbles or tennis balls, they're usually fireballs."

Mini-Travis's jaw goes slack. "No way."

"Sorry," you say.

Mini-Travis goes off, shaking his head. You expect Travis to disappear, too. But he lingers.

"Where'd you learn all this stuff?" he asks.

"Some in school and some from the pair-o-rents." You jerk your head toward the Bird Woman and Mr. Nature Man, who are busy studying ancient graffiti. Only here it's called petroglyphs. "They're like serious nature freaks."

"Cool. It's awesome to know so much."

You blink. Did you hear him correctly? Did Travis just say that being a nature freak was cool? Did he just say knowing all this useless stuff was awesome?

"So what's your name?" he asks.

"Sierra."

Travis glances at the tree huggers with their day packs and hiking boots. He smirks. "Yeah, figures. Think you'll be back at the beach tomorrow?"

"Sure. What about you?"

"Definitely. We'll go snorkeling, and you can tell me what some of those fish are, okay?" He starts to go back to his group.

You're in a daze. Tomorrow? At the beach? He wants to

go snorkeling? So . . . he doesn't think you're a geek or a freak of nature?

"Wait," you call behind him.

He stops and looks back.

"So what's your name?" you ask.

"Bob."

Bob?

Well, it's not Travis, but it'll definitely do.

Over spring vacation of 2001 family friends and I took our children to an "environmentally sensitive eco-resort" in the Caribbean. The kids ranged in age from twelve to eighteen, four girls and one boy. The three adults on the trip consider themselves politically correct. Indeed, the one mother among us owns and runs a company that oversees ten day-care centers. We are sticklers about sunblock, preservation of reefs, and equality in all matters regarding the sexes. We work hard to instill these values in our children. But not always with success, especially where the younger members of the group are concerned. Such enlightenment, I suspect, may, in some cases, come with age.

Todd Strasser

Todd Strasser is the author of more than 100 novels. His books have won numerous state, national, and international awards and are available in many languages.

His most recent novel for older teens and adults is the controversial *Give A Boy A Gun*, an investigation into the circumstances surrounding a fictional school shooting. His books for younger teens include *Thief of Dreams* and *Con-Fidence,* as well as several popular series for middle-grade students: the Help! I'm Trapped in . . . books, the Don't Get Caught books, as well as the Heavenly Litebody and Against the Odds series.

Todd has worked as a newspaper reporter, advertising copywriter, and magazine journalist. In 1978 he sold his first novel, *Angel Dust Blues* and used the money to start the Dr. Wing Tip Shoo fortune-cookie company. For many years the fortune cookies helped him live while he wrote more books.

Todd now divides his work between writing books and speaking at schools and conferences. When he's at home, he likes to spend time with his children and dog, Mac. He enjoys fishing, tennis, and surfing.

Angel & Aly

Ron Koertge

With her blond hair and blue eyes, my sister looks like her name: Angel. And actually, I'm kind of like my name, too: Mona. Get-the-job-done Mona. Mona with one skinned knee and hair that doesn't get in the way.

We're twins, but you'd never know it by looking at us. Angel was 100 percent totally recycled, environmentally friendly: granny glasses, Birkenstock sandals, as vegetarian as possible. The idea that a cow got bonked on the head just so she could eat a burger was too much for her. She cried when we passed McDonald's, which helps explain why she weighed about eleven ounces.

I'm mostly REI: soccer shirts, mountain bikes, and a taste for El Grande burritos with lots of hot sauce. I'm a rock-solid eighty-seven pounds. I am Mona, hear me roar.

But that's not the story. Aly. That's the story.

First, some background. Our parents were amazingly distracted. Zoned. Elsewhere. Mom was a pediatrician (still is), and Dad worked at the jet propulsion lab (still does). But he used to say to people he was meeting for the first time, "I'm in space." That was his only joke. *Uno*. The lone jest. And it wasn't that funny because it was so true. At breakfast he'd eat anything I put in front of him: cornflakes, leftovers from La Salsa, a pork chop. It didn't matter. He was "in space." Ha-Ha. Mom? Pretty much the same. She was probably on the phone saying, "If it goes over one hundred and four, take her to the ER, and I'll meet you there." To them, the dining room was just a place to refuel and then get back out there. All they needed was a pit crew.

Picture us at breakfast: Mom's on the phone; Dad's sketching some trajectory or other. Angel is frowning at the pan on the front burner.

I say, "It doesn't hurt the oats." I put frozen waffles in the toaster. "Or the wheat that made these."

She sticks her tongue out at me. "I'm not that nuts."

"You're pretty nuts."

My sister frowns at her juice glass, the one with clowns on it. "Only about the air we breathe, the ground we stand on, the water we drink."

"Yeah, yeah. You'd like it if the guy who grew those oranges stood underneath the tree until they were ready to fall off, wouldn't you? You wish he'd catch them wearing cashmere gloves, don't you?"

"You think you're so smart, Mona."

Mom puts the phone to her sweater, smothering it. "Don't fight, girls."

We look at each other and shrug.

It's a relief to get out of the house. Except when Angel walks to school, she keeps her head down so she won't step on a bug. I have to be right beside her the whole way; it's like babysitting Helen Keller.

When we get there, I make sure she's got her homework, not that it matters because it's only half done. On purpose. Angel's smart. She could cream anybody in the science fair, for instance. But she won't enter because, and I quote, "If I win, somebody has to lose." So she gets C's. Sabotages herself to get them, too.

I put lunch money in her purse and make her promise not to give it away.

Finally, I get to say hi to my friends on the soccer team and to see what's what. We trade some homework, get the lowdown on last night. Some pathetic boy goes by on a skateboard and crashes so we'll be impressed.

None of that lasts long, though, because somebody runs up and tells me Angel's getting picked on again. As usual.

So I trudge across the schoolyard. When I get to the scene of the crime, the kid takes one look at me and slinks away. I put one arm around Angel's skinny shoulders.

"See where that Mahatma Gandhi crap gets you? On the ground with some pimply troll calling you a tree hugger."

"Violence consumes our hearts, our homes, and our societies. I'm not going to be part of that."

"He took your lunch money!"

"I don't mind sharing."

So you get the picture. That Was My Life. Before Aly. Who came into the picture by accident when Mom brought home a hand puppet from the hospital.

Now, I know this sounds kind of charming: Overworked pediatrician buys her supersensitive daughter a little something from the gift shop and whispers, "I know I've been busy, dear, but I'm always thinking of you." Get serious. Here's how it really went down.

Mom's standing in the foyer, still in her cashmere coat (she's busy but well dressed). She's got it half off when her cell phone rings. She pats the pockets: Out comes a hairbrush, a set of keys, half a pack of Dentyne gum, a hand puppet, a phone. Then, "Blah blah blah, fever, blah blah blah, MRI, blah."

She sees me. "Mona, how are you, honey?"

I decide to amuse myself: "I'm addicted to crack, and my boyfriend steals cars."

"Did I call you about dinner, or did you call me?"

Non sequitur, thy name is Mother.

"You called me. I defrosted hamburger. We'll eat in about fifteen minutes."

"Where's your father?"

"Orbiting Mars."

She holds the coat with one hand and starts putting

things back like a pickpocket unclear on the concept. "What's this?"

She shows me an alligator hand puppet: long green head, yellow eyes, white felt teeth, half a sleeve for a neck.

I just shrug.

Mom examines it, turns it over a couple of times. "Must be Juanita's."

"And Juanita is . . . ?"

"This little girl we lost today. I was in her room all morning." Mom sighs. "I think I'll have a glass of wine. Do you want something?"

"New parents would be nice."

Mom smiles. A little. She's thinking about Juanita. The dead girl. That's the business she's in—saving people, making them better. Except she can't every time. And then she has to answer her cell phone anyway. And do paperwork at the hospital anyway.

Which explains, I guess, why she can't remember who called who about dinner. Suzanne Boland's mother stays home, grows tarragon in pots, grinds flour for bread, and generally makes Martha Stewart look lazy.

Are these the only options? Isn't there anything in between? It all makes me want to live with wolves.

I point. "Give the alligator to Angel. She likes that baby stuff."

"Pardon me?" Mom sits straight up. All she heard was *Angel* and *alligator.* I could have said Angel was eaten by an alligator.

I repeat myself. "That hand puppet. Give it to Angel. Your daughter. Remember?"

"Oh, all right. Where is she?"

"I'll get her."

Angel is in her room. On one wall she has a map of the world with different-colored pins for trouble spots—gray for dwindling elephant populations, red for fires in the rain forests, yellow for outbreaks of malaria. That sort of thing.

She's sitting cross-legged, palms up on her knees. Her World Wildlife Fund T-shirt is grimy. She doesn't like to do laundry because she's worried about the water table. Me? I think the water table needs four matching chairs.

I tap on the open door. "What are you doing?"

"Visualizing world peace."

"Well, put it on the back burner for a minute. Mom wants to see you."

"Really?"

I admit it: I'm Mona the Teenage Cynic. I think *It's a Wonderful Life* is a stupid movie, Britney Spears embarrasses me, Jewel's poetry sucks, and worrying about which boy likes who how much is a complete waste of time.

But the way my sister says "Really?" gets to me. God, she's the bunny in the crosshairs, the baby on the ice floe, the turtle on the freeway.

I lead her down the carpeted stairs. Angel runs, puts her head on Mom's knee. Mom's hand leaves her wineglass and works through some tangles in Angel's hair.

A Kodak moment for sure if our completely distractible mother hadn't been looking at me with *What's this all about?* written across her forehead.

I head for the foyer, pick up the hand puppet, trudge back to the kitchen.

"Look what Mom got for you."

Angel sits up. "Really?"

That again.

"I love alligators!" Angel runs her hand right up the sleeve, wriggles her fingers into place, snaps the jaws a couple of times.

"They're hinged on the bottom, see?" She shows us by making that part move. "Like us." She makes a few chomping sounds. "They're threatened but not endangered anymore. Thanks, Mom. This is great. I love it. Say thanks, Aly."

Is that when it started? I barely noticed that she'd named it. What's to notice? It was a kid's name for a kid's toy, like Oxy the octopus or Annie the anaconda.

"Aly," she repeats. "Say thanks."

Aly takes everything in with those beady eyes: the copper-bottomed pots hanging from the rack over the stove, the big double-door Amana refrigerator, the table we eat breakfast at. It looks down at the sea green tile, then at me. Those yellow eyes narrow. Seem to narrow. It tilts its head a little. Its mouth opens. Then closes.

I check out my sister, holding Mom's hand, putting the back of it against her forehead like she's pretending to have a fever. Angel's turned away from Aly, like she's got nothing to do with it. The puppet—I know how weird this sounds—kind of has a life of its own.

Just then the phone rings. Mom reaches for the blue Nokia that she's stashed beside the little vase full of pencils. But before she can get it and push the Talk button, Aly goes for her. Gets her wrist between his jaws and holds on. Holds on tight.

"What in the world?" Mom tries to shake the puppet off. "Angel! Stop it!" The phone keeps ringing. Mom struggles with Aly. Angel just stares out the window like none of this is happening.

Mom picks up, finally, but with her left hand. Twitching slightly, her right one lies on the counter with Aly's jaws locked around it.

Of course she gets away—it's just a hand puppet—then scowls at Angel and stalks into the other room.

I ask my sister, "What was that?"

"What was what?"

"You grabbing Mom like that."

"I didn't grab Mom. Aly did."

I look at the stupid puppet. Who looks back. Who opens its big, red mouth.

I tell her, "You're making it do that."

Angel shakes her head.

"Oh, yeah? Well, take your hand out of there and see what happens."

She obliges. Aly lies there, not much bigger than one of Dad's socks.

I point. "See? Aly doesn't do anything on his own." I

correct myself. "Its own." I don't want to get into that whole gender thing with a piece of cloth.

Angel says, "Aly needs me, but I don't really do anything." Her hand disappears into the green sleeve. Aly turns to me slowly and—I've got to admit—kind of hypnotically. I think of those movies about India, those swaying cobras.

And then Aly says something. I mean, it's Angel. I know that. Her mouth even moves. But so does Aly's. And Aly's voice is different than Angel's little vegetarian, piccolo voice. This one is deeper, raspier.

"It's like electricity," Aly explains. "I'm plugged into Angel."

"Uh-huh." I have two choices: freak out and call the exorcist, or play along. "So what do you guys want for dinner?"

Angel says, "I'm having rice because that's what political prisoners eat."

"I'll have zebra," says Aly.

I look puzzled. "Gee, I'm pretty sure we're all out of zebra."

"If you want to go get one," Aly advises, "what you do is wait for them to wade into the shallows to drink and then grab 'em by the muzzle, pull 'em in, and drown 'em. But you have to be patient."

I look at my sister. She usually hates that tooth-and-claw stuff. She can't watch anything on the Animal Channel except kittens playing in a basket. Angel is oblivious again.

I say, "I'm not wading into anything."

"Cow, then?" asks Aly.

I nod. "Hamburger."

Aly sighs. "It'll have to do."

I was the cook. Sort of. We've got a housekeeper who comes in while we're at school, at the hospital, and in orbit. She cleans, does laundry, makes dinner and leaves it in the fridge.

But if something needed doing, I did it. Toss a salad. Heat some rolls.

I've already said how my parents are no-nonsense eaters. They file in when I call them. Angel usually chews one grain of rice at a time and slumps like she's been beaten by cruel, godless captors.

But that night is different. Not that Mom notices. She's probably thinking about Juanita. What else she might have done. Or how there was nothing else to do. She calls this "looking into the void." So she does that.

Dad has got months of work sitting on the launchpad in Florida with a cracked bolt. Forget him.

But I notice. Angel is eating hamburger! When she's not pretending to squint into the blinding light of her interrogators, she's attacking that hamburger patty!

I can't believe my eyes. She eats the whole thing. And she's not dainty, either. No morsels for her. No tidbits. She picks up the burger, Aly nods eagerly, and then she wolfs it down. Makes big, chewing noises. Aly burps. Then Angel burps. This is some weird proxy eating.

Mom frowns. "Say 'Excuse me.'"

Aly says it, then lies down on the table and goes to sleep. Angel eats another grain of rice.

As usual, I make the rounds at bedtime. Check the doors and windows. Turn off the lights. In my parents' bedroom, Dad is asleep, curled up in a little ball. I like to look at him with his glasses off. When I was little, I never played with dolls or had a tea set or any of that girly stuff. But I liked to tuck my dad in. I still like it. One hand sticks out from under the maroon bedspread. I lift it carefully and put it under the yellow sheet. I tug at the covers, make sure his shoulders won't get cold.

Mom's sitting at her vanity taking off her makeup, not that she wears much. She's in her underwear. Just a bra and a pair of basic underpants. Her skin is warm. I lean into her.

"Everything okay?" she asks.

"Are you kidding? Your daughter's talking to an alligator."

"Now, Mona. Don't pick on your sister. She's never been as mature as you."

"I'm not kidding, Mom. I think you and Dad ought to—"

She stands up. "Can we talk about this tomorrow? I'm just exhausted."

So I go check on Angel. She's asleep, but not in the middle of her bed like always. She's against the wall. Aly is right beside her; she's left room for him. Like he was really there. All six scaly feet of him.

The next morning, I plead with my parents. "Tell her

she can't take that dumb thing to school. First it was Tupperware with Tofu, then it was Vegans for Victory. Now a hand puppet? My friends are going to fall down laughing."

Mom takes the phone away from her ear. "Sweetheart, don't embarrass your sister. Leave Sally at home."

"It's Aly."

"Yes, well, leave him at home."

"All right."

But she doesn't. She disobeys. I can't believe it.

So we start toward school as usual. Except things aren't as usual. Forget the bugs; they can take care of themselves. She's got Aly. He's looking around. Checking everything out. His long head scans left, then right. He and Angel talk.

"Where's the swamp?" he asks.

"Behind the school," says Angel.

This knocks me out a little because it's a lie. Not a big one, I admit. But Angel never used to lie. It was part of who she was: no meat, recycle/reuse, give part of her allowance to Habitat for Humanity, et cetera, et cetera. And no lies.

On the other hand, she's just lying to a puppet. Does that count?

"What's school?" asks Aly.

"It's where we go to learn."

"Learn what?"

"How to add and how to read. There's things to memorize. Stuff like that."

"Can we swim and get covered with mud and lie around in the sun?"

"No."

Aly says, "It sounds boring."

"It is."

"Angel, what are you talking about?" I stop them. Wait—I stop *her.* "You like school."

Aly turns to me. "Who asked you? Butt out."

When we get to school and come to the place where the sidewalks meet, the place where we always say good-bye, I tell her, "Maybe stash that thing somewhere until school's over."

She looks at me. Aly does, too. "Why?"

"You're thirteen and you're playing with a toy."

"I'm not a toy," growls Aly.

"He's not a toy," says Angel.

"Got your lunch money?" I fuss with my sister's back-pack, the one with the whale logo. I push at her silky hair.

Aly looks at the three dollar bills. "More," he says. "I could eat a horse."

"Please," says Angel.

I give her a five. "Hide it."

"She's safe with me," says Aly.

I go and talk to my friends. There's all kinds of news. The goalkeeper on our soccer team thinks she's too fat, so she's making herself throw up after she eats. Another girl has a date with a sixteen-year-old boy. Who has a car. And a bad reputation. I'm listening. I'm also waiting for some kid to come get me: Angel's crying, or Angel's getting picked on, or somebody took Angel's favorite pencil, the one from the Humane Society.

But nobody shows up. One of my friends has a new cell phone. Another one calls her; they're like five feet apart. They're talking way too loud about where anybody can buy marijuana.

I tell them, "I'll be right back."

I'm almost to the science building when I hear it. Kids cheering. Yelling Angel's name. I round the corner. There's a brat named Sean who always picks on Angel. I look for him first.

Guess where he is. On the ground. With Angel straddling him. With Aly biting at him. Sean's batting at the puppet, but Aly is everywhere the kid isn't.

I rush up and grab my sister, pull her off. She's light, so I swing her around, put myself between her and Sean, who's bawling like the little weenie he is.

"You okay?" I guess I expect her to cry. Show some remorse, maybe.

Instead, Aly shakes himself. "That was fun."

"Stop that!"

"Stop what?" asks Aly.

"Not you." I wrap one hand around his jaws. He struggles a little, then doesn't.

"What happened, Angel?"

"Aly was just protecting me. You know how Sean is."

"You don't fight. You don't believe in fighting."

"Aly fought."

"Yeah? Well, you're the one who'd get detention."

"I'm hungry," says Aly.

Angel looks at the vending machines. The same ones she picketed with a sign that said STOP CORPORATE CALORIE TERRORISM.

Aly leers at me. "Angel said something about a Baby Ruth. I could eat a baby named Ruth."

Great. A bloodthirsty puppet.

I've got this big project in chemistry, but even that makes me think about what's going on with Angel. I mean, it's like these three or four elements are getting along fine making oxygen or coal or whatever. Then along comes another one and *boom*! Everything's destabilized.

Aly's the new element. Or Angel is. The new Angel. The one who eats a lot. A lot of meat. She gains some weight. Kids at school don't pick on her. She starts sleeping in class right beside you-know-who, but her grades go up anyway.

Sometimes Angel says she wants to walk to school by herself, and that makes me feel weird. We *always* walked together. I know I complained about it, but I liked it, too. More than I knew, I guess.

I miss the old Angel. The idealistic one. The one who was nice enough for both of us. And now that she's not so nice anymore, I'm sort of starting to think I should be. A little, anyway. I mean, what about those girls I told you about: the almost bulimic one, the going-out-with-older-boy one? What'd I do but soak up the gossip and then be glad it wasn't me? I should have said something. Okay, they probably wouldn't have listened to me, but that shouldn't have stopped me from trying.

Then we're having dinner one night when Aly leans into me.

"We're going to Florida," he hisses.

"Who is?"

"Angel and me. You got any money?"

I look around him at my sister. "Are you kidding?"

"Aly wants to see a real swamp."

"You can't go to Florida by yourself."

"I'd never go by myself. I've got Aly. Interesting people will give us rides."

Then she tears into a pork chop, and I mean tears. She's got it between her teeth. Aly chomps away, his big dirty jaw right beside Angel's. And she's going, "Arggh! Arggh!" She's growling and tossing her head, shaking the pork chop like it's trying to get away.

Mom looks at me and says, "What is wrong with Angel?"

That's when I snap. I go off like one of Dad's rockets. I start yelling.

"I tried to tell you what's wrong with Angel. I tried that night when I said she was talking to a puppet. But oh, no—you were exhausted. Well, now look: She's about to hitchhike to Florida, and you haven't got a clue about why. God, Mom—stop saving other kids when your own are going down for the third time!"

That gets her attention. She looks at Dad, who's got a forkful of salad halfway to his mouth. She reaches for me. "Mona, honey."

I'm on my feet. The chair goes over behind me. "And you never come to my soccer games. And when you do, you're always late, and then somebody calls and you turn your back and talk. I cook, sort of, anyway. I for sure stack the dishes. I lock the doors and turn down the thermostat." Then I look at my dad. "There's not a launch every day. I'll bet you just sit at your desk a lot, like everybody else. I know you're not used to paying attention to your kids, but you're wrong. We're not doing too good without you."

And then I cry. I can't believe it. I never cry. Not when I broke an ankle last year, not when I get knocked down in soccer or dive for a volleyball. But I can't stop crying. And then Angel starts. She puts her thin arms around me, and we both bawl. On each other. By the time we stop, we're as wet as orphans in the storm.

My parents are just pale. We don't finish dinner but have a little powwow instead. They actually try to listen. They say they're sorry. Angel promises she won't go anywhere. She keeps Aly in her lap, out of sight.

Of course, later on, when she and I are supposed to be asleep, we hear arguing about who neglected whom the most. And why. Then about who's going to be on duty when. And the phrase "She's your daughter, too" gets used more than once.

The very next day, Mom gets a deal on phones. Mine is red, Angel's green. Alligator green. But I see less and less of Aly. He doesn't go to school every day. He doesn't always eat with us.

Mom phones us regularly. For no reason. Just to say hi. At first I'm like, Oh, sure. Just wait. But she doesn't forget. She invites us to lunch at the cafeteria at the hospital. She takes us shopping. Together and separately. I know it's corny, but I like it.

Angel still eats a lot of steak. She's got new friends now, but some of them creep me out. School bores her; Mom has to sit right beside her or she won't do her homework. Dad and I watch videos: *The Right Stuff, From the Earth to the Moon, Beyond the Stars, 2001: A Space Odyssey.* Over and over. But I don't care. It's nice to sit beside him with his arm around me. Across the room Mom turns the pages of Angel's history book, points to something, and they both laugh.

I think of Aly, upstairs in the corner with Curious George, just another toy.

I was born and raised in southern Illinois, and it was just Southern enough to have pockets of old-fashioned fire and brimstone/hellfire and damnation. And lots of thou-shalt-nots.

But I was drawn to everything my pastor said I was not supposed to do or to like. Dancing was frowned upon, but I was a good dancer. Swearing was taboo, but I liked all kinds of words. Movies were a bad influence, but I loved (I still love) movies.

Just like in my story, I was both Angel and Aly: pious and sensitive, rude and crude.

Of course, this is a grown-up's distillation of those years. In general, I got along fairly well with my sometimes bewildered parents, had friends and girlfriends, got my heart broken, played basketball, looked forward to getting my driver's license.

But I also knew I would never live in my hometown, never settle down there. I didn't so much know what I wanted but only what I didn't want. My friends seemed very sure of themselves (as only thirteen-year-olds can), but not me. Sometimes I wanted to be selfless, to help people, and to make the world a better place. Often, though, I wanted to do nothing but have a good time and banish the shaming voices of the congregation. Even at thirteen, though I couldn't have put this into words, I understood that my church was a political organization, that its main goal was self-preservation, and that it sold a kind of sameness that was not in my best interests.

That last sentence is the kind of thing Aly would say, if he could talk. He can't. He's a hand puppet. And I made him up.

But that doesn't mean he isn't right.

Ron Koertge

Ron Koertge is the author of many award-winning books, like *The Arizona Kid* and *Tiger, Tiger, Burning Bright*. His most recent novels for young adults are *The Brimstone Journals* and *Stoner & Spaz*. When not writing, he is usually at the racetrack, trying to find the fastest horse to bet on.

Nobody Stole Jason Grayson

Carolyn Mackler

I've only stolen two times in my life. The first time was when I was in fifth grade and my dad sent me to Wal-Mart for vacuum-cleaner bags. I slipped a jumbo box of Sour Patch Kids under my windbreaker and ate the entire thing on the walk home. It left me with stomach cramps and a raw tongue.

The second time was last Monday, when I swiped a picture of Jason Grayson out of Daytona McCauly's locker. I'd had a crush on Jason since the beginning of the school year. Despite his rhyming name, he's the most popular guy in junior high. So naturally, he went out with Daytona, eighth-grade diva, most likely to be on the cover of *Teen People*, most likely to diss you if you see her in the grocery store.

But the whole popularity thing wasn't why I had a crush on Jason. It was his eyes. They're a warm ambery color with long reddish lashes. Not that I ever got a close look at them. But my locker is two down from Daytona's, where she and Jason would cuddle and coo between every period. I got ample opportunity to watch him looking into *her* eyes to imagine what it would be like if he gazed into my pale grayish ones.

On Monday afternoon, I was twenty-five minutes late getting to my locker. It was all because of my earth science teacher. We were doing this lab on surface runoff, and he matched up the lab partners but forgot to put me with anyone. I had to stay after school to do the extra work.

The halls were empty by the time I made it to my locker. I'd just finished loading up my backpack when I noticed that Daytona's locker was cracked open. Upon closer inspection, I realized that a hair band was preventing the door from fully closing. I scanned the halls to confirm that I was alone and then peeked into her locker.

I saw it right away. Among the postcards of palm-treed beaches and pictures of her fifty-seven best friends forever—all taped to the inside of her locker door—I glimpsed a snapshot of Jason Grayson. It was in the top right corner. It must have been taken last summer because his skin was as tan as a new penny.

I know that stealing is wrong and immoral and can give you stomach cramps and a raw tongue, but as I gazed longingly into Daytona's locker something inside of me couldn't stop thinking, I want—no, I *need*—that picture of Jason Grayson.

I unstuck the small squares of tape, slipped the photo into my earth science textbook, nimbly closed her locker, and scurried out of school.

Little did I know that this minuscule misdemeanor was going to touch off the most turbulent week ever known to Valley View Junior High.

As I lay on my bed that evening, I could hear my dad vacuuming in the living room. My dad used to be the world's biggest slob, which my mom always complained about until six years ago, when she packed her bags and left. That's when my dad became a neat freak. He barely has time for anything else since he spends four hours a night and every weekend scrubbing and dusting and mopping our spotless home.

I propped a pillow under my neck and pulled the picture of Jason out of my textbook. I tried to imagine what it would be like to kiss him, if we'd use our tongues or if it would just be light pecking. It looks like he and Daytona are all about their tongues. But Daytona wears at least a B-cup, so she's a completely different story.

Me, I'm a nobody. There's nothing distinctive about me. I've never done anything special in my life, nothing that would make me stand out. Even my name is bland. Abby Tad.

I'm at the bottom of the food chain in school. Right down there with Sloppy Joe. His real name is Joey Neidermeyer, but he got that nickname from the time in kindergarten when he was carrying a sloppy joe across the cafeteria. He tripped and dropped his tray. As the reddish-brownish mystery meat sploshed across the floor, kids pointed and laughed. No one really calls him Sloppy Joe anymore—just a few bully types—though I still think of him like that in my head.

He's sort of a loner, like me. I have a few friends. Not *friends*, really. More like girls I sit with at lunch or on a field trip. But it's not like we chat on the phone or swap school gossip or even talk that much, really.

I sighed heavily and rolled over on my side. It's hard being thirteen and still flat-chested and still too embarrassed to ask my dad to buy me a razor so I can shave my legs. As I stroked Jason's face, I pretended that he was my boyfriend, who loved me regardless of my nonexistent boobs and my nonexistent social status.

I could hear Daytona's voice before I even turned onto our hallway the next morning.

"Where's my picture of Jason?" she was shrieking. "Do you think someone stole it?"

As I got closer to my locker, I spotted Brooke and Kylee, two other junior high divas, hanging out at Daytona's locker. Brooke's glossy lips were mashed together, and Kylee was fiddling with her charm bracelet.

"Hold on," Daytona said sharply. "You're the only people who know my locker combination. Maybe one of *you* took it."

Kylee yawned and paddled her palm over her mouth. "Maybe it fell out," she said.

"Maybe the janitor swept it up," said Brooke, sliding on another coat of lip gloss.

"I don't believe you." Daytona jabbed her finger in their faces. "I'm going to tell my dad, and he'll make sure whoever stole it gets punished big-time."

Daytona's father is Mr. McCauly, the vice principal of Valley View Junior High. She's got him wrapped around her manicured finger. If you've read *Charlie and the Chocolate Factory*, he's Mr. Salt to Daytona's Veruca.

"Fine," scoffed Kylee. "Go ahead and tell Daddy."

"Who would want to steal your stupid picture, anyway?" added Brooke.

They both strutted away, propelling their hips from side to side.

By lunchtime, word of the stolen photo had spread through school. That's all people were talking about. That and the fact that Daytona and Kylee and Brooke had had a catfight in the hallway. As I sat at my regular table, eating a tray of curly fries and not talking to my nonfriends, I thought about how Jason's photo was hidden in my earth science textbook. That's when I got this unfamiliar jumpy feeling inside—partially from nerves, but partially from somehow being at the epicenter of all this action.

That night, my dad went to Wal-Mart to buy a bottle of Old English oil. When he got home, he told me how he ran into one of his coworkers in the checkout line.

"I heard there's been some trouble at Valley View," my dad said as he daubed the furniture polish onto a rag.

"What do you mean?" I asked.

"Dave Jacobs told me that his son said items were being stolen from lockers."

I was in the middle of making a peanut butter and honey sandwich for dinner. I jabbed through the bread with my butter knife.

"Just be careful with your new backpack, Abby," my dad said as he began rubbing the polish on the inside of a cupboard door.

The next day was Wednesday. When I arrived at my locker, Daytona and Jason were embroiled in an intense discussion.

"I don't understand," Daytona whined. "How could the photo have just disappeared like that?"

"Why are you freaking out?" Jason kicked his sneaker against a locker. "I mean, you can take another picture of me. I'll bring in my mom's camera tomorrow, if you want."

"I don't want another photo," Daytona said, her voice growing shriller. "I want *that* photo!"

Jason glanced around uncomfortably. "Chill, Daytona. It's not a big deal."

"Not a big deal?" Daytona shrieked.

"Look," Jason said, "I'm sick of the way you always freak out about everything. It's getting a little old. Until you calm down, I don't think we should see each other anymore."

Jason started down the hallway.

"I am calm!" Daytona shouted after him, but he didn't turn around.

Daytona slammed her locker so hard that my earth science textbook toppled to the floor. I stared down at it, praying Jason's photo wouldn't slip out of the pages.

The next thing I knew, Sloppy Joe—who must have been walking by—bent over and scooped up my book.

"Express delivery," he said, handing it to me.

I smiled. "Thanks."

As I put the textbook back on the top shelf of my locker, I decided I should probably find a safer place to stash the stolen photo.

The next morning, I dug a safety pin out of the medicine cabinet and fastened the photo to the inside of my jeans, near my pocket. The corners poked into my skin, but I liked having Jason so close to me.

I was lucky I did that because as soon as I arrived in homeroom, Mr. McCauly's voice came over the loudspeaker.

"Attention, students," he said, clearing his throat. "Due to a recent incident, the principal and I are doing a random locker search this morning. We're instructing everyone to remain in homeroom until further notice."

By 10:30, we were allowed to go to our normal classes. They obviously hadn't found the photo, but they did discover a pack of cigarettes in a seventh grader's locker and some small bottles of rum tucked into an eighth grader's gym sneakers. Both kids were suspended for two weeks.

If that weren't drama enough, a fight broke out during sixth-period art class. We were doing a unit on batiking fabric. We were all stationed at the sinks, with torn-up white sheets, melted wax, and bottles of dye. Before I knew it, Daytona started elbowing Brooke. Brooke shoved Daytona. Kylee, pretending to break it up, rubbed wax on Daytona's eighty-dollar jeans.

Mr. McCauly was summoned. As he threw himself into the ruckus, an open bottle of pink dye flew into the air and landed on the vice principal's snow-white hair. He trucked toward the bathroom, beads of fuchsia trickling onto his shoulders.

On Friday, while Mr. McCauly was consulting a hair specialist about removing the pink coloring, the principal called every student into her office, one by one, to see what they knew about the stolen photo. I was in the last group of kids, right at the end of the day. It was just me, Sloppy Joe, and this sixth-grade girl who's legally blind *and* was absent on Monday. I guess we're the nobodies, the people least likely to do anything remotely suspicious.

I ran my hand along my khakis, where the photo was pinned inside my waistband. That's when the door opened and Jason Grayson walked into the waiting room. After having him so close to me this past week, I was starting to feel like I actually knew him. I raised my hand to wave, but I did it so quickly that a folder slipped from my lap, sending papers fluttering onto the gray industrial carpet.

I could swear that Jason muttered "Dork" under his breath as he handed a manila envelope to the principal's secretary and walked out again.

My eyes stung. This is not how Jason Grayson, boy of the amber eyes and long lashes, was supposed to act.

Sloppy Joe got on his hands and knees and gathered my stray papers.

"Express delivery." He grinned as he set the pile of papers on my lap and returned to his chair. "I'm becoming your regular postman."

"Thanks," I said, smiling.

As I stuffed the contents back into my folder, I glanced over at Sloppy Joe. I never noticed before that he had a dimple in his chin. Maybe it only appears when he smiles.

I was just deciding that it was about time to stop thinking of him as Sloppy Joe when the principal appeared in the doorway to her office, surveying her clipboard.

"Abby Tad."

I took a deep breath and followed the principal into her office. I settled into the chair facing her desk as the secretary beeped her. "Bert McCauly on line one," he said over the speakerphone.

The principal held up her hand, instructing me to wait, and lifted the receiver to her ear.

"Yes, Bert, any luck with your hair?"

Silence.

"Four more weeks? Oh no. I'm so sorry."

More silence.

"Yes, I'm questioning the last group of kids. . . . No, no . . . it's nobody, really. I'm afraid we'll have to wrap up this investigation . . . write it off as an unsolved mystery."

Nobody?

"You're wondering what you'll tell Daytona?" the principal asked into the phone. "Just tell her that nobody did it. Nobody stole Jason Grayson."

Nobody stole Jason Grayson. Something about the way she kept saying *nobody* bothered me. I almost wanted to stand up, rip the photo out from inside my khakis, and shout, "Don't be so quick to call someone a nobody!"

As soon as she hung up, she crossed one knee over the other and said, "So, Amy, do you know about this missing photo?"

"My name is *Abby.*" I clenched my jaw. "And I don't know anything about it."

That's when it hit me. I'm sick of being a nobody. I'm sick of people not remembering me. And I'm sick of Jason Grayson. For all I know, he wears color contacts.

That evening, I unpinned the photo from my pants, sealed it into an envelope, and scribbled onto the front, *Don't open until I'm fourteen.* I'm hoping by then I'll make better choices about who I have crushes on. I slid the envelope under my mattress and headed into the living room. If I helped my dad clean, maybe he'd have more time to spend with me over the weekend and maybe I could ask him to buy me a training bra or a pack of those pastel razors that I see girls using in gym class.

We were spritzing Windex on the windows when the phone rang. My dad headed into the kitchen. I smiled as I worked the paper towel in circles. It's kind of relaxing to wash windows. Besides, my dad just said he'd take me out for pizza tomorrow as his way of thanking me. Pizza Hut *happens* to be across the highway from the mall, so maybe that'll be the first step in my acquisition of a certain undergarment.

"Abby?" he called out. "It's for you."

I set my paper towel on the windowsill. "For me? Who is it?"

"Someone from school."

I walked into the kitchen and wedged the phone between my ear and my shoulder.

"Hello?"

"Abby? It's Joey."

"Joey?"

"Sloppy Joe," he said. "Your personal postman."

"Oh," I said, laughing out loud. I paused before adding, "You shouldn't call yourself Sloppy Joe."

"Do you like 'Postman' better?"

"How about just Joey?"

"I've always wanted to be Just Joey," he said.

I cracked up again.

Joey was quiet for a moment. "I called to tell you that after you left the principal's office, I found your school ID under a chair. I can give it back to you on Monday if you want."

"Monday's fine," I said. "Do you want to meet me in the lunch line?"

"Sure. I'll buy you some creamed corn."

"No," I said. "It's my treat."

Joey laughed. "Oh, boy. Do you really mean it?"

After we hung up, I thought about how I don't regret taking Jason's photo. It's not like I'm going to make a habit out of petty thievery, but when I think about how much has happened these past four days, it strikes me that maybe I'm not a nobody anymore. I mean, nobodies don't disrupt an entire school and receive phone calls from cute boys with dimples in their chins.

From now on, I'm going to think of myself as a recovering nobody. I don't know what my future will hold, but I can guarantee one thing: It won't be nothing.

The summer after eighth grade my best friend, Shamira, invited me to join her family at their time-share condominium in the Bahamas. Shamira had been my Siamese twin since we were toddlers, but she had recently moved from our small town in western New York to Bowling Green, Ohio. While I had remained with a tame group of friends—all-girl slumber parties, lusting after boys without daring to make a move—Shamira had shot ahead socially. She reported back from the Midwest with tales of designer jeans and coed parties and French kissing.

Summers for me have always been a time to break away, to take risks, to get out of ruts—and that week in the Bahamas was prime opportunity. On several balmy Bahamian nights, following Shamira's lead, I got vamped up in a strapless dress and plenty of blue mascara.

Pretending to be eighteen, we sneaked into casinos and played the slot machines. I lay by the poolside, slathered in tanning oil, and listened to the song "American Pie" for the first time. I wore short shorts and a straw hat. I watched Shamira flirting with boys and took copious mental notes.

There was one guy at the condo named Darren. He was nineteen, Canadian, blond, and the sexiest person I'd seen in my entire life. While Darren had better things to do than hang out with thirteen-year-olds, I did *manage to exchange a few words with him, enough to get him to pose, tanned and shirtless, for a picture.*

Upon returning to western New York, I went to a pool party and brought along the picture of Darren. Like Abby in "Nobody Stole Jason Grayson," just carrying his photo made me strut with newfound confidence. Unlike my main character, I flaunted the picture to my oohing and aahing girlfriends, instantly increasing my social standing.

Later that summer, after I turned fourteen, I made out with my first boy and got my first period. So that week in the Bahamas will always be what thirteen is about to me—when I dipped my toes into teenagedom without fully diving in, when a picture of a guy was almost better than the guy himself.

Carolyn Mackler

When Carolyn Mackler was thirteen, she wrote in her journal, "Someday I want to be an inventor, a child-care worker, a teacher, an actress, and lots of other things." Fourteen years later, she published her first teen novel, *Love and Other Four-Letter Words*, which was praised by literary critics and selected by the American Library Association as a Quick Pick for Reluctant Young Adult Readers. Carolyn's second teen novel is *The Earth, My Butt, and Other Big Round Things*. She frequently writes short stories for *Girls' Life* and contributes to *Teen People, Seventeen,* and *Glamour*. Not yet an inventor, a child-care worker, a teacher, an actress, or lots of other things, Carolyn lives in New York City, where she's working on a new novel.

Tina looked at the piece of paper the Queen handed her. "Why is Maia difficult?" she asked.

"She just doesn't get it," said the Queen, looking tired.

"Doesn't get what?"

"The big deal. She doesn't understand why turning thirteen is special. She thinks tomorrow is going to be like any other day in her life, except that she'll have a cake. She thinks she'll still look the same, feel the same. She'll go to the same school with the same friends. She doesn't think anything is going to change, at least not for the better."

The Queen glanced down and studied her wand for a moment. "Maia is rather skeptical and recalcitrant. She's a rationalist, with her feet planted firmly on the ground. She likes numbers, facts, and scientific evidence. She doesn't believe in magic or wishes or dreaming about the future. To her, thirteen is just a day more than twelve. Do you think you're ready for this assignment, Tina? We usually dispatch you to the easier sells."

"I could sell teenhood to the Tooth Fairy," said Tina. "Make her want to leave the Tooth Force and come work for us."

The Queen looked sharply at Tina. "You have only one chance. It's tonight or never."

"I know, I know. I've done this hundreds of times."

"Off you go, then." The Queen moved to the next fairy in line.

Tina looked at Maia's address once more, then waved her wand and disappeared.

Tina the Teen Fairy

Ann M. Martin and Laura Godwin

Tina the Teen Fairy stood outside the entrance to Teen Land, awaiting her instructions. She was 954th in a line of thousands of Teen Fairies, but she was not concerned about the wait. Time in Teen Land moves at a pace of its own. Tina would have her instructions shortly, and then she could get on with the evening. She snapped her gum, smoothed her yellow bell-bottoms, and adjusted her wings, keeping them free of her Woodstock T-shirt.

"Tina!" a voice called.

"Here!" Tina stepped out of the line and stood in front of the Queen Teen Fairy.

"We have a particularly difficult assignment for you tonight," said the Queen.

"Okay," replied Tina. "I'm ready. Who is it?"

"Her name is Maia Grant. She lives in Port Hill, New Jersey. Here's the address."

The house at 429 Glen Road in Port Hill was dark. Tina, who had shrunk to the size of a speck of fairy dust, floated through the screen in Maia's window. Then she enlarged herself until she was the height of a quarter and perched on Maia's pillow, waiting for midnight.

When the clock struck twelve, Tina enlarged herself again, this time to Maia's size, and stood by her bed, shaking the girl's shoulder.

"Just five more minutes, Mom," mumbled Maia. "Let me sleep."

"It's not your mother, it's me, Tina the Teen Fairy. And you have to wake up right now and come with me." Tina turned on Maia's reading light.

Maia sat up, rubbing her eyes. She blinked at Tina. "I must be dreaming," she said.

"Nope. You're not dreaming. See my wings? You can touch them."

"What?"

"My wings." Tina spread her wings as wide as they would go. "They're real. In fact, we can't get to Teen Land without them. Now come on. We don't have much time."

Maia opened her mouth to scream.

Tina was prepared. She waved her wand over Maia, and in a flash the house on Glen Road was below them, and Tina and Maia were soaring high above Port Hill.

"You can't do this to me!" Maia cried. "I'll sue you. My parents will sue you. I have rights!"

"Maia, for heaven's sake, calm down," said Tina. "Just

listen to me for a minute." Tina paused, and when Maia didn't say anything, she went on. "You're Maia Grant, and you're turning thirteen tomorrow, aren't you?"

"Yes," said Maia.

"Well, all right, then."

"All right what?"

"I'm here to take you to Teen Land, indoctrinate you into teenhood. This happens to everyone the night before their thirteenth birthday. Everyone in the world. A Teen Fairy visits at midnight, takes you to your own special version of Teen Land, shows you around, answers your questions, and delivers you back to your bed before you wake up."

"If this happens to everyone, how come I've never heard of it?"

"Because people don't remember their trips to Teen Land. That's part of the magic. But believe me, everyone who's older than twelve has been there. Even your parents."

"If you don't remember the trip, what's the point?"

"You don't remember the trip itself," replied Tina patiently, "but the Lessons of Teen Land are stored in your subconscious."

"Well, if we get these great lessons," said Maia, "then how come all teenagers aren't—"

"Oh, look! Here we are!" cried Tina. "Get ready to slow down now."

"The only reason," said Maia as she and Tina coasted over a large gateway with TEEN LAND spelled out in lights, "that I'm going along with all of this is that I *know* it's a dream."

"Whatever works for you," said Tina. She executed a smooth landing in a grassy area in front of a brick building with TLS etched over the doorway.

Maia looked at the kids swarming in and out of Teen Land School. She looked at a mall across the way, at a side street lined with tidy houses, cars parked in the driveways, and at another street with rows and rows of high-rise apartments. "This is supposed to be Teen Land?" Maia said. "It just looks like anywhere in the good old U.S. of A. Except that"—Maia eyed Tina suspiciously—"some of the people here have wings."

"Those would be the Teen Fairies," said Tina. "The others are pre-fairies. They haven't earned their wings yet."

"Where are the grown-ups?" asked Maia. "And the little kids?"

"There aren't any. This is Teen Land. Didn't you see the sign?"

Maia ignored the question. She turned her attention to Tina. "So what's with the outfit? You look a little . . . old-fashioned."

Tina grinned. "I'm from nineteen sixty-nine. I'm something of a hippie."

"What's wrong with *this* year? You have a problem with now?"

"You know, missy, you have a pretty bad attitude." Tina snapped her gum. "And you're not going to learn anything tonight unless you drop it. What's the problem? You don't like my wings? You don't like our little land here? What?"

Maia sighed hugely. "Look. I am not the one who flew into someone's room, woke her up, and dragged her into some weird teenage dream. I didn't want to turn thirteen in the first place, and—"

"Aha!" cried Tina. "I knew it! Now we're getting somewhere. Come on. Let's go to the malt shop and have a chat."

"The *malt* shop?"

"Yes. It's run by a bunch of teens from nineteen fifty-two. It's one of my favorite hangouts."

Tina led Maia beyond the school to a row of shops and restaurants. She sat her at a table in the back of Sadie's Place and ordered two chocolate sodas. "All right. Now, why don't you want to turn thirteen?" she asked Maia.

"Because it's bogus. Everyone makes such a big deal about it. Like, 'Oh, now you're thirteen. You're such a young lady.' Or, 'Ooh, Maia, you're practically an adult.' Like I'm going to wake up tomorrow—if I ever get out of this dream—and I'll be transformed. But it's not true. What's going to be different?"

The waiter brought their sodas then, and Tina unwrapped her straw. "Haven't your parents told you that you can have more privileges or anything?" she asked.

"Yeah. Now I can stay up until eleven on school nights and eleven-thirty on the weekends. But that's just the point. Do my parents have bedtimes? No. And that's because *they're* the real adults. I'm turning thirteen, but *I* still have a bedtime, *I* still shop in the junior department, *I* still go to the pedia*tri*cian. I can't vote and I can't drive, but I have to pay full price at the movies. Plus now I'm expected to get an after-school job, but it'll hardly be worth the teeny amount of money I'll be able to earn since I'm only thirteen. I'm not really a kid, and I'm not really an adult. It stinks."

"Huh," said Tina.

Maia sipped her soda as she looked around Sadie's. "So these teenagers," she said. "I mean, these pre-fairies or whatever they are, these fairies without wings. Who are they? Like, who's that girl coming in the door? The one wearing the sign. What does it say? 'Save the Whales'?"

Tina glanced up. "That's Activist Teen," she said. "And the two kids behind her are Vegetarian Teen and Volunteer Teen. They've stuck with those roles for pretty long. Lots of kids change roles more quickly. See Fashion Model Teen over there in the corner? She tried that role for a week or so, and now she's ready to switch. I think tomorrow she's going to try being History Buff Teen."

"What do you mean, they change roles?"

"Well, they experiment, just like real teenagers do. They're finding out who they are, seeing what they're good at, what they enjoy, what's meaningful to them. While they're growing, their wings are growing, too. That's what your teen years are for, you know. Growing and experimenting. And making mistakes is part of that."

"Yeah?"

"Yeah. Are you done with your soda? Because if you are, there's something I want to show you. Come on."

Tina left a tip on the table and led the way out of Sadie's, thanking College-Bound Teen for holding the door open for them.

"Where are we going?" asked Maia, running to keep up with Tina.

"To the library. I think you'll find this interesting."

The shelves of the Teen Land Library were lined with videotapes, nothing but videotapes. Tina waved to Librarian Teen, who was sitting behind the front desk, then led Maia to a particular shelf and ran her finger along the videos there until she came to #283760, with a date from twenty-five years in the past. Under the date was the word *Hair.* "This should be it," murmured Tina as she removed the tape from its case. "Okay, Maia. Come to the screening room with me. Let's take a look at this."

In the screening room, several bewildered kids were seated in front of monitors with their Teen Fairies, watching videos. Tina slid the tape she had chosen into a VCR and pressed the PLAY button. Maia found herself looking at a young girl leaning over a sink, busily dying her long red hair jet-black. The girl raised her head.

"Hey!" cried Maia. "That looks like my mother."

"It is your mother. I mean, it was."

"I never saw her with black hair before."

"That was an experiment," said Tina. "Also a mistake. Your mother was in Phase One of Self-Experimentation."

"What was Phase Two?"

Tina fast-forwarded the tape. "Here we go," she said.

She pressed the PLAY button, and there was Maia's mother, her hair now much shorter and dyed bright pink with a blue streak down one side.

Maia's mouth dropped open. "That was for Halloween, right?"

"Nope. First day of school, tenth grade. Let me show you eleventh grade."

Maia peered at the next image on the screen. She saw lots and lots and lots of red hair. "Where's her face?" she asked.

"It's in there somewhere."

"You know, I wanted to dye my hair green, but Mom wouldn't let me."

"Maybe she was remembering Phase Two," said Tina.

"It still doesn't seem fair."

"Well, you're right. It isn't. Your mom just wants to protect you, though. It may not work, but she means well. Classic Parent-of-Teen Mistake. The point is, your mom did some experimenting when she was a teen. So did your dad. So did your grandparents. They experimented. They made mistakes, and they learned from them. And now your mom wants to pass on her hard-won knowledge to you." Tina looked at her watch. "We don't have a lot of time left," she said. "I have to get you back home before your alarm goes off."

"Can we watch another video before we leave? I want to see my dad make a mistake."

Tina grinned. "All right, but quickly. And then I want to show you one more thing."

Tina slid another video into the VCR, and she and Maia watched it intently.

"My dad played in a garage band? He wanted to be a drummer? But he's terrible! Listen to him." Maia was incredulous. "And look at his clothes! And . . . and . . . is he wearing an *earring*?" Maia hooted.

A few minutes later, when Tina and Maia left the library, the sunlight was fading. They walked past the Teen Land School again and along several streets in town.

"The truth is," said Maia quietly, "I don't know what I want to be. I hate when everyone asks me that question. 'And, Maia, what do you want to be when you grow up?' Like, how should I know that now?"

"I agree," said Tina. "It's an impossible question. But what kinds of things do you like to do?"

"I don't know. I like painting, I guess," said Maia as they passed a girl setting up an easel.

"You should try being Artist Teen for a while."

"What if I don't like it?"

Tina shrugged. "Then try something else. That's what this time is for, these next few years. It's not quite as easy to experiment when you're an adult. Most people have too many other responsibilities then."

Tina stopped at a road that led out of town. Enormous weeping willows let their branches down over either side of it. Above flew bluebirds. Butterflies lazed from flower to flower. At the end of the road the sun was setting, a great red ball.

"Wow," said Maia. "This is beautiful. Like an air-freshener commercial. Where does that road go?"

"That's the road to adulthood."

"*Adult*hood? But I want to walk down the road *now.*"

Tina turned Maia around. "And miss all that?" she said, gesturing toward Teen Land. "Time to paint? Time to spend with your friends? Time to figure out who you are? Time to dye your hair? You want to waste all that and head on down the road already? You're going to get there eventually, Maia. Don't wish this time away. You don't get it back, you know."

"Well, I might like to try being Artist Teen for a while," said Maia.

"Great," replied Tina. "And if it isn't for you?"

"Well, I had this idea for a pet-sitting service."

"Oh, Small Business Teen," said Tina. "Very clever. All right, Maia. I'm afraid we'd better leave now. I have to get you home quickly." Tina waved her wand, and in a flash she and Maia were in the air again.

They whooshed over Teen Land and through the early morning sky to Port Hill. As they approached the Grants' house, Tina said, "You aren't going to remember this adventure, Maia, but I'm going to do you a favor and plant a suggestion in your subconscious. It will come to you at the appropriate time."

"What is it?"

"Ask your mother to tell you about her pink hair."

Maia grinned at Tina, but before she could say anything, Tina waved her wand again and Maia disappeared from her side. A moment later she was asleep in her bed. Her alarm clock would go off in five minutes.

Tina the Teen Fairy, the size of a speck of dust, spread her wings and soared upward, thinking about the report she would write for the Queen. "Happy thirteenth birthday, Maia," she whispered as she flew back to Teen Land.

We had such different experiences as teenagers that it was hard to create a story that rang true for both of us. Ann grew up in the college town of Princeton, New Jersey, not far from New York and Philadelphia. Laura grew up in the farming community of Olds, Alberta, in western Canada. Ann took all her studies seriously, whereas Laura had a more selective approach to school. Ann's interests were in quieter, solitary activities such as needlework. Laura, on the other hand, enjoyed all sorts of team sports, including curling! However, when it came to turning thirteen, both Laura and Ann shared many of the feelings Maia has in the story. Neither liked answering the question "What do you want to be when you grow up?" And both were just as happy if the adults left them alone. It was this common ground, and their mutual appreciation of humor, that led to the idea of a visit from the Teen Fairy.

Laura Godwin

Laura Godwin was born and raised in Alberta, Canada. She is the author of several picture books and early readers, as well as the coauthor, with Ann M. Martin, of *The Doll People.* She lives in New York City.

Ann M. Martin

Ann M. Martin is the author of the Baby-Sitters Club series, as well as eighteen books for middle-grade readers, including *The Doll People,* written with Laura Godwin; *Belle Teal;* and *A Corner of the Universe.* She lives in upstate New York.

Atheneum Books for Young Readers
An imprint of Simon & Schuster
Children's Publishing Division
1230 Avenue of the Americas
New York, New York 10020

This book is a work of fiction. Names, characters, places, and incidents are either products of the author's imagination or are used fictitiously. Any resemblance to actual events or locales or persons, living or dead, is entirely coincidental.

Book design by Polly Kanevsky and Alex Ferrari
The text for this book is set in Fairfield.
Printed in the United States of America
First Edition
2 4 6 8 10 9 7 5 3 1
Library of Congress Cataloging-in-Publication Data
13: Thirteen stories that capture the agony and ecstasy of being thirteen /
edited by James Howe.— 1st ed.
p. cm.
ISBN 0-689-82863-2
1. Teenagers—Juvenile fiction. 2. Short stories, American.
[1. Teenagers—Fiction. 2. Short stories.] I. Howe, James, 1946-
PZ5.T3195 2003
[Fic]—dc21 2003012802

"Such Foolishness" was previously published in 1992 in *Kalliope: A Journal of Women's Art.*